BUSTED ON BROADWAY

WAYNE CLARK

Published by Wayne Clark YUL/NYC

ISBN: 978-1-7780739-4-6

Cover and book design: Nell Chitty

PI Humph Barstal first appeared in
One Murder Too Many,
available on Amazon.

ACKNOWLEDGEMENTS

The author would like to thank
Meghan Clark-Combot and Barry Clark
for their encouragement and insightful assistance.

In memory of Bob Stall

CONTENTS

CHAPTER 1

HUMPHREY Barstal was once the name on the private detective's business card. Since achieving fame of sorts in 1927 for solving a front-page crime involving kidnapping, international bootlegging, Wall Street scamming, forced prostitution and murder, the *New York World* newspaper that followed such matters began to know him as Humph. Humph himself preferred it that way. So much was his fame now, six years later, that his new cards simply read, "HUMPH, PI." He hated being called Humphrey.

His apartment, tiny for such a big man, was a nondescript tenement on Henry Street on the Lower East Side, in the shadow of Chinatown. It was zoned residential and did not allow commercial signage. However, Humph had an artist friend in the East Village who offered to design him an almost discreet Humph PI plaque to affix to his downstairs mailbox. Beneath the words was a sketch of his oversized head sporting an undersized bowler hat. The artist's sketch resembled those seen in the *New Yorker* magazine, minimal strokes conveying subtle humor. The artist worked for free. His dad was a former cop like Humph.

Humph appreciated the price. Crime hadn't stopped since the Great Depression had taken root in America but fewer victims had the wherewithal to seek help beyond a call to the cops. The police themselves were limping their way through the motions of protecting New Yorkers. They had abysmal salaries to begin with and their numbers had been severely amputated by city hall. Humph lived cheaply, so cheaply that the young woman he called his daughter-in-law, Eve, never missed a chance to chide him about his needless frugality.

Eve wasn't actually his daughter. She was the daughter of a woman named Sunny, the one and only woman Humph had ever loved. She was murdered years ago. The crime snuffed out the life of one of New York's better-known burlesque performers. When she died, Humph stepped in to protect her daughter, Eve. Now, in her late 20s, Eve reciprocated. Humph was her father in more ways than she could count. She knew even as a child how her mother regarded the giant cop. They were from worlds at the opposite end of the universe but they loved each other. Not that she tried but her mother could never have hidden that fact.

Nowadays, Eve looked after Humph as much as he looked after her, especially when she'd been kidnapped six years earlier and forced to dance in gangster-owed clubs and perform a striptease for favored customers in a private room. It was Humph and a rising star in the police department, a female officer, who lived to break down barriers for women. That was the spirit of the 1920s and she wore the pants to prove the new world for women wasn't going to go away.

Almost from the get-go, Eve hoped Humph would marry her but it didn't work out. For a while, in the glow that followed their solving one of the biggest cases in NYPD history, it looked like they might. Humph even took her on a winter vacation to Miami. Neither said much on their return, except that the weather beat

New York's. Both of them disappeared, neck deep in new cases. Eve began to think her father would never marry. He was too damned idiosyncratic to make room for another human being day and night.

But Eve had reason to worry about him. She knew he hadn't had a big case, one that paid big, in months. The country was reeling. One in five men were out of work, maybe more. And just the other night the radio said the Great Plains were being swept away by oceans of dust flooding the skies and obliterating crops and homesteads with a fierceness that only God-fearing people could put a name to. America was being punished, they said. The moneylenders' temples were toppled. Greed was being swallowed up. The survivors ate dirt and seeds and insects. In their prayers, they prayed for the strength to forgive Wall Street. Sadly, they admitted, the howling dust storms outside were too loud for them to hear whether their prayers were being answered.

Eve was not religious in the slightest. Since she first started performing in burlesque shows and stripping between shows as a teenager, she knew the reality of New York streets put the lie to the existence of any kind of overseer god. There were good hearts and people with no hearts.

Humph wasn't religious either. An orphan, he was raised by a Jewish couple who taught him to be open to every faith. As a result, he ended up not hating anyone or any group in particular, which the Christian churches especially seemed to foster, a point driven home when they parleyed their hatred of demon rum and those who drank into a nationwide law that declared America dry. Prohibition. It gave birth to more crime than the country had ever known.

Thanks to his parents, Humph grew up as a reader, which almost none of his friends were. He was thoughtful by nature, and tried to remain that way when he put on a too-small uniform as a rookie New York cop. Almost anyone could become a cop, it seemed. He was probably hired for his size, more than six feet tall with a head so big it could surely survive a lot of knocking about on the Bowery, near where his first precinct station was located.

Humph kept in touch with Karena, the female cop who rescued Eve and almost rescued his soul. The tone of their conversations was always warm but he confined his calls to inquiries about possible clients in cases the NYPD was having trouble solving.

Karena was his major contact now but the NYPD's Women's Bureau didn't necessarily know all the big cases the force was dealing with. I didn't occur to male cops to keep the ladies in the loop.

In the past, Humph had a pipeline of police information, thanks to a rarely sober but tenacious Irish cop named Duffy, the kind of flatfoot they don't make anymore, Humph thought. Duffy broke all the rules of investigation, spat on procedures and took it upon himself far too often to inflict justice himself. But by God he got results. For his work on Humph's big case, he got promoted to detective. Sadly for Duffy and Humph, the promotion brought along with it an independence of action that too often led to benders of Irish proportions. A year and a half ago, he was relieved of his duties but without prejudice. The Irish army on the force extended all the way to the top echelons. They had to fire him but in the eyes of most he was one of the great boyos.

Humph thought so, too. His visits to Duffy's rooms on the Bowery near Grand Street were fraught with danger, not physical danger but if Humph was planning to get any work done that day Duffy's insistence on sharing a bottle for old times' sake obliterated all such intentions. When Duffy was still a cop, Humph felt he tried harder to toe the line, but now that he was no longer representing the force, Humph figured he had a right to live as he wanted. That was how Humph lived already and why marrying the pretty Ukrainian cop would never have worked out.

As Humph leaned against the windowsill and looked down on passersby, and picked out the cries of street vendors, all of whom he knew after more than a decade at the address, he heard a loud tattooing at his door.

It was Eve. She entered, tucking herself under his right arm so he could hug her. Before he released her, she swatted his belly with a rolled-up newspaper. It was that day's *Daily Mirror*.

"Look at the first page," she ordered. Humph sat and obeyed.

"What am I looking for?" he asked.

"The story about the actor."

"Where?"

"Here!" Eve's eagerness to show him the story now had a tinge of impatience with her dad's plodding ways.

Still holding the paper in front of his face, he looked up at Eve's face and laughed. He had been teasing her and her notion that he was becoming a fuddy-duddy. She forced herself to keep a straight face and pointed again at the headline. "Look!"

"DeLawd assassinated."

"Lawd?"

"Yes, DeLawd. The Lord, if you will. God Assassinated. DeLawd is a character in what was the biggest hit on Broadway a couple of years, a show called *The Green Pastures*.

"What was it about?"

"I'll tell you later. What matters right now is this murder," Eve said.

"Why? What's so special about murder in New York?"

Eve was getting seriously agitated. She wanted cases for Humph.

"There's talk, Dad. Lots of talk. At first everyone, including the cops, thought he was killed just because he was black. Read the story. His name was Joel Jean-Baptiste.

Near the bottom, there's a quote from an unnamed cop. He said, 'He was probably rubbed out because someone thought he was too big for his britches.'"

"What nonsense," said Eve. "The show ended two years ago and as I said he was just an understudy. Actors knew him and to have been chosen as understudy for DeGawd, he must have been a marvel on stage. But the general public wouldn't have known that."

"I'm positive the murder wasn't racist, Dad. There's talk. Talk everywhere. A woman was involved, a rich one."

Humph knew that Eve was in a position to know. After the kidnapping, she vowed she would never return to stripping. She'd had a lifetime of degradation thanks to gangsters. Since her release, after the nightmares stopped, Eve decided on a career change. She already knew how to dance and sing. She knew how to play to an audience. She was pretty to boot.

"Broadway, here I come," she announced to Karena one afternoon at the police officer's apartment. Humph was due to arrive later. Eve had to run but Karena couldn't wait to pass on the news to Humph.

Because of Eve's mother, Humph had learned to like theater. He still went from time to time but the sight of a stage usually stabbed at his heart until the show got underway.

Eve, as independent of spirit as he was, had spent a year and a half auditioning for shows. The process left her exhausted and desperate to learn tricks about staying positive.

Her introductory card read, "Dancer, actress, singer. Professional." The high point of those 18 months was the fact that she got several call backs before the final chop. The other auditioners told her that was miles better than most got. They said, "Keep at it, girl." And she did, earning her rent money waitressing at a diner on Delancey. A couple of years before, when she lived nearby, she used to eat there. The staff knew she was a burlesque performer and treated her like the down-to-earth star she was. Eve knew she wasn't a star. She was usually just a fill-in. But the make-believe was too good to destroy.

Now she was on Broadway. It was a minor role but one that sent her résumé into the stratosphere. At future auditions she would get first crack, like the other pros.

Humph was so proud of her that he never said a word about her success. But he beamed at her a lot for no apparent reason. So much so that people noticed.

"Dad, this case is not what it seems." Before announcing that, Eve plunked herself down on the floor right in front of Humph to make sure she got his full attention.

"How so?" Humph asked.

"As I said, there's a woman involved, Dad. A rich woman. But the article doesn't mention her."

Humph reread the newspaper article. In the end, there were few facts and too many presumptions on the part of the NYPD. Black men got killed without their deaths usually being recorded by a newspaper. Most of the cops were less than thorough when investigating them. The papers preferred high-society murders, white murders, and the intrigue behind gangster corpses. Maybe this particular murder had a story worthy of a little ink.

It was the kind of investigation Humph liked. Years ago, when the *New York World* gave him a press card signed by the chief of police to help him give the paper an exclusive on the bootlegging-kidnapping case, Humph started to see investigations not just as a private eye but as a reporter. His newspaper career ended quietly when his inability to type proved to be more than inconvenient for both himself and the paper.

"Surely," Humph said to Eve, "the star of a hit show, black or white, would get the full attention of the police department."

"But," said Eve, "if you read to the bottom of the

story, you'll see that the murdered man was not the star of the show but his understudy. The star of the show is alive and well. I've met people who know him. He's not even American. He's from London. Not England, London, Canada, London Ontario. The guy who was murdered is from Newark."

Eve let Humph digest the information. After several minutes, he replied.

"The only reason to kill a guy nobody knew, like an understudy, was either a jealous fellow actor or an outsider with another axe to grind. But as you said, the show closed in 1931. I somehow don't think this was a racist killing."

Eve leapt to her feet and hugged Humph.

"Yes, yes, yes. That's just what I think. That's why we're the best detectives in the world."

"We?"

"Well, you know what I mean," Eve said.

Humph smiled and said that if she weren't a big star on Broadway he'd hire her as a partner.

"Maybe someday, when my dancing gams grow weary."

CHAPTER 2

EVEN though his pal, Duffy, had retired, Humph still made it a habit to drop by the old precinct to sniff around for potential cases. Most private dicks wouldn't be able to elicit half the tips Humph got. Not only was he once one of their own, he was now almost famous and the ones who were around at the time of the case liked to think they basked in the same light. Humph had been a good cop, a cop's cop, they liked to say.

Humph viewed his uniformed past a little differently. They thought he was a cop's cop not because of anything he did. All he did was keep his mouth shut about whatever happened in that little police station on a poorly lit street on the Lower East Side. He never spoke up about the over-enthusiastic interrogations. Most of all he kept his yap shut about the bootlegging business they ran from the basement.

No cop at that precinct ever paid for booze during the long run of Prohibition. They merrily confiscated the alcohol from speakeasies and somehow forgot to pour it down a drain or a sewer. Their collection of drinks was getting so large they had started getting picky about what types and brands of booze they confiscated during raids.

A couple of his old buddies had their own thoughts about the case of the murdered understudy. After all, his corpse was found within walking distance of the precinct, something the cops always appreciated. They both said the murder was "a delicate one".

"When is murder ever delicate?" Humph asked.

"When the man has lipstick on his face and a razor thin cut across his throat. No signs of struggle. The apartment, his, was entirely in order. In fact it was pristine, like it had been scrubbed with Brillo pads."

"A female kind of spotless?" Humph wondered.

"Yeah. Exactly. Something a dame would do."

"In fact, we even found a cloth soaked with blood in the waste can. We think maybe the killer used it to soak up the blood spurtin' from his gizzard, you know, to protect the carpet."

"Any idea who the woman could be?"

"Nope. Not a clue."

"Thanks, boys. That's a big help."

"How?"

"Don't know yet but I now know more than what was in the police report. I've got an angle to kick around."

"Glad to help, Officer H."

Humph's next stop was the office of the *New York World*, on Park Row, a pleasant walk away on a fresh winter morning. His friend there, Gerald Franklin, was no longer a cub reporter. He had risen through a long stint on the city desk and found himself anointed crime features editor, a newly created post. The paper had realized that the majority of its readers were meat and potato readers, who loved to chomp down on murder and mayhem, and above all else, stories pulling the rug out from under the rich and famous.

Humph wouldn't admit it but he shared the paper's priorities, and in this case, the one based on Eve's suspicion, the latter part, the demolition of the rich and famous.

All of America was wheezing under the weight of the Great Depression. For a privileged few, the Twenties still roared in the new decade.

Franklin was a man of facts, just like Humph. When he was with Franklin, Humph understood why Eve said he was a plodder, a most frustrating, kill-joy plodder. Humph was feeling the same way now about Franklin.

"If I understand you, Humph, despite the fact that you have no real evidence, you think the murderer of this actor, Joel something or other, was a wealthy woman, maybe even a member of our so-called high society. But you have no idea who she might be."

"Right. But I don't know anyone in those circles and, forgive me, I don't read your gossip columnists."

"You should," said Franklin. "They know a lot more than they write. The rich and famous hate them but at the same time they know they can bludgeon their careers or social standing. God bless the First Amendment, Humph."

Franklin said it with a smile but Humph thought it was the best part of the Constitution.

"A lot of our society ladies go stir-crazy, Humph. One the one hand, they know they are held in esteem solely because of the wealth of their husbands. They go through the motions of blessing the downtrodden with charitable pursuits but they have no damn idea who those downtrodden are or even why they are downtrodden. Beyond their make-up, they do nothing every day. That's not easy on anyone. There's little to do but get fat and keep smiling alongside dear old hubbie before the assembled Chamber of Commerce worshippers."

"You've opened a door, young man."

Franklin smiled, knowing damn well that Humph was not ready to tell him which door he'd opened.

Almost whimsically, he tossed Humph some more bait.

"Recently, we even discovered that a lady of some standing in our fair metropolis once approached a Broadway director and, citing her and her husband's importance, insisted she be given a role as a singer. The director graciously had a piano player summoned. The musician let the lady explain to him what song she wanted to perform. She chose the syrupy *My Blue Heaven*. The director shrank in his seat before finally waving his arms frantically to put an end to the torture. Miss Society Lady didn't exactly get kicked in the nether regions as most upstarts would have been, but she was dismissed in no uncertain terms. Once home on West End Avenue, she called her lawyer and insisted he launch a lawsuit against the producer and director. Her lawyer shared the director's opinion of her but her money left him tone deaf as it were."

"Name and address," said Humph. "You're a magician, Franklin."

Before Humph had a chance to leave the building, Franklin steered him against the wall at the entrance and said:

"Old friend, I won't ask what case you're working on. I only want to know if you'd like to continue using our resources and whether..."

"I know, I know, I know," interrupted Humph. "You want to know whether you'll get a scoop."

"You're a man of few words, Humph. As a word man myself, I appreciate that. And yes, scoops get me raises."

As he exited to the street, Humph tapped him on the shoulder. Humph intended it as a friendly gesture but Franklin, who stood 5-foot-8, winced. Sometimes, Franklin thought, the big guy just couldn't help himself. In the end, it was an endearing characteristic. Franklin knew the feat Humph pulled off to solve the 1927 case that had left the entire NYPD baffled. It was as if naysayers weren't tall enough to send a message through Humph's ears. He just kept shoving his way forward in the case.

Later that night, Humph called Franklin at home.

"If I ever unearth anything about this actor's murder, I'll let you know before anyone else, Franklin. Just spell my name right, and for Christ's sake, the name Humphrey can never appear in your paper. It's Humph or nothing."

The next stop was going to be Broadway, where Jean-Baptiste last performed, the Eugene O'Neill theater on West 49ᵗʰ. But Humph wanted to get prepped by Eve, who was performing only blocks away, at the city's westernmost Broadway Theater on Ninth Avenue, the Al Hirschfield Theater. Humph's head was spinning with the list of theaters he'd gotten from Franklin. Some he'd heard of, like the O'Neill. He'd never heard of Eve's theater even though it was a major vaudeville theater when his Sunny was performing.

When he got there, he looked at the marquee and hoped to see her name. It wasn't there. She was just a dancer-singer who joined the chorus when another dancer was ill or injured. But the theater entrance looked grand to him. My girl should be living in a house like this, he thought. His reverie was snuffed out when a woman's voice asserted: "Your ticket, sir?"

"My daughter is in the show. I need to see her before she goes on."

"I'm sorry, sir. It's too late for that. If you'd care to wait in the manager's office until the end of the show…"

"No," said Humph. "I'll see her at home."

Inexplicably, Humph felt sad as he made his way back to Seventh Avenue. He had no reason to expect that he could see her whenever he wanted but he felt hurt. A few blocks later he realized he had to accept his little girl, now almost 30 years of age, wasn't a little girl. She was an adult, a courageous one, carving out a life in what must be the world's most difficult city in a profession that most newcomers would give up on within a week. A few blocks later, the realization settled in that even though she wasn't a star, she was a survivor. That made you a New Yorker.

It was possible, he decided by the time he reached the Bowery, that she had more balls than he did. What she went through…that was a hell Humph had never faced. Yet whenever she entered his place, there it was, that goofy smile. Women weren't what they used to be. Or maybe, they weren't what men thought they used to be.

When he stepped into his flat, he found a note on the door.

"Her name is Samantha Sidwell. Call her at the number I gave you. Say you are a Broadway agent and that someone told you she had a voice that should have been discovered years ago. Don't worry. She'll see you, guaranteed. Franklin."

Eve called Humph just before midnight.

"Can we talk later? I don't have a job anymore. After tonight's show the producer walked into the dressing room…half of us were nude, Humph!…and he said, just as if he were saying the breakfast special is blah-blah, the show has folded. It's over. It's dead. I'm dead. I don't know. Can I see you tomorrow morning? I'm going to get drunker than any woman in New York has ever gotten. If I can see straight, I'll drop by tomorrow, Dad."

The next morning, Humph phoned Eve. No answer. Had he reached her he would have told her he couldn't see her that morning. He was sure that she would have rejoiced in the news.

Humph had already made an appointment to visit Mrs. Samantha Sidwell, a woman whose noggin was likely as off-key as her singing. She agreed to see him the next afternoon. Humph used the morning to go to the library to see what he could find under the name Sidwell.

By the time he left the library, he knew that Sidwell, an investment banker, had once produced an off-Broadway show. By the time Humph got back to his apartment, he'd already forgotten the name of the musical as had most New Yorkers. It ran for only 32 days. Humph couldn't help wondering whether his wife insisted on auditioning for that show, too. Maybe he decided to swallow the financial hit and close the show just to put an end to her hounding him for a role and risk having even more ridicule being heaped on the show.

Humph's research turned up a gossip column from one of the *News of the World* competitors that quoted Sidwell as saying his business hero was Joseph P. Kennedy, Sr., one of the handful of men whose wealth exploded during the early years of the Depression. He made millions using insider information and manipulating the market anyway he could. And why not. It was an unregulated market. Kennedy then decided that the stock market was overvalued. For him, that was an opportunity. He sold most of his stock holdings before the crash of 1929 and made even more money by selling short, betting on stock prices to fall. Humph only learned about these shenanigans while investigating his 1927 case, the one that started with the son of a rich capitalist being swindled out of $10,000 by an illegal bucket shop just off Wall Street.

Humph's library research also informed him that in the 20s, Kennedy gobbled up failing Hollywood film companies that made schlock films for the most part and made them more efficient. He then sold them, walking away with another $5 million.

Humph wondered whether Sidwell's hero had inspired him to try his hand at the entertainment business as well, this time the Broadway version. Regardless, this information might provide chat possibilities when he met the litigious Mrs. Sidwell that afternoon.

Once home, Humph felt tempted to call Karena. She could help him dress appropriately for West End Avenue.

After a few minutes of daydreaming, he realized he couldn't. They were over as a couple. She was at work and she'd made it clear her work was as important as his. Haberdashery help was no longer on the menu.

He was resigned to being himself. It was not something he felt difficult to do normally but something told him his investigative chances would be improved by not appearing as a total outsider to Mrs. Sidwell's world.

Humph buffed his shoes, verified the crease in his pants, and reached into the closet. Without looking into the closet, his hand found a hat, one he'd never worn. Eve all but forced him to buy it. It was not his usual bowler. It was a fedora. She even showed him how to wear it.

"It has to be at a slight angle. It will make you dashing, Dad, even rakish should the occasion demand. Try it. Try it."

He did. At first he didn't recognize himself. He was about to say No when Eve said, with great hyperbole, that "You are the face of the modern New York City private eye." She added, "You have to look like you just walked off a movie set."

When Humph remembered her comment about the movies, he opted for the fedora. It wasn't until he got to the subway that he looked in a train window while going through a dark tunnel and adjusted the angle. Afterwards, he looked around the crowded car but nobody appeared to have noticed his moment of vanity.

CHAPTER 3

AT the door of the apartment, he was let in by a butler who took his fedora. Before putting it on a closet shelf, he flipped the brim slightly, assuming that was the look the visitor wanted. It was certainly the look Eve had wanted.

Humph was led into a drawing room. At the far end, from a few feet above floor level to the very ceiling was a painting in fashionable art deco style of two women, bodies touching each other lightly, both gazing silently at occupants of the room. Rather than sitting in a fragile chair—they all appeared to be antiques—-Humph opted for a sofa. There were two facing each other on opposite sides of the room. The back of his faced a window. He hoped the annoying light might make Mrs. Sidwell join him on the sofa, opening the door to a more intimate, confidential interview.

As Humph surveyed the room, the butler returned to announce that Mrs. Sidwell would present herself in approximately four minutes. Such precision, thought Humph. Why wouldn't he have said simply, "about five minutes"? The butler added that "She has suffered a contretemps of sorts, sir." Nice word, "contretemps", thought Humph. He wondered if Mrs. Sidwell had broken a fingernail.

Humph profited from the time to rise and examine a music stand in the far corner, to the left of the overbearing art deco ladies on the wall. The title of the sheet music was *My Blue Heaven*, the very song that sunk her audition.

At last, Mrs. Sidwell arrived. Although Humph half expected she would, she didn't flounce in. Instead, she presented herself as a lady.

"A pleasure to make your acquaintance, sir. I always value having the opportunity to interact with representatives of theater and the higher arts in general."

Unable to fashion a smarmy smile in recognition of her pat praises, Humph bowed his head.

"Mrs. Sidwell, I'm told you are a practitioner of the vocal arts." As soon as he said that he wondered where in the hell that wording came from.

However, he got the desired reaction.

"Ahem, well, yes, you could say that. I can claim to do a little more than merely dabble."

"Well, I'm sure you know Broadway has become the lifeblood of New York and we need to devour talent wherever we find it."

"Oh, yes, I do understand. My husband, Mr. Sidwell, you must know already that he has been a Broadway producer. The theater is in our blood, you might say."

Knowing the background to their involvement in Broadway, Humph struggled to find an immediate and polite response. The question he knew he must ask was the one he most wanted to avoid.

"Could you perchance perform a tune or two for me to give me an idea of where your voice might best find a home in one of my shows. I'm producing three at the moment. They are in various stages of preparation but one is already weeks away from going to Toronto to test audience response. Right after that, it will set up shop in Philadelphia, just a stone's throw from New York and the unforgiving eyes of our newspaper critics. It's all very exciting, of course, Mrs. Sidwell, but each day we hire and fire, so to speak. We are after nothing but the best."

Humph had learned about the process from Eve. It was brutal for actors, dancers and singers, and brutal for the money people.

Amazingly, Mrs. Sidwell did not shrink from the standards Humph had outlined.

"Allow me, sir."

With measured steps, she approached her music stand, which was located next to a piano. Turning it to face Humph, she picked up her sheet music and appeared to give it a quick read-through.

"Did you bring a pianist, sir?"

"No," Humph replied. He started to stutter, then suddenly brought a perfect response to his tongue.

"A Capella is the gold standard for voices, madam."

"Of course, of course," Mrs. Sidwell responded. Humph noted that her answer was less enthusiastic than her previous ones.

A moment later, Mrs. Sidwell announced that she would sing the song in Bb instead of Eb, the key in which it was written.

"I can transpose, of course. My voice is true enough for that, but I feel you will feel my song more if I do it in Bb."

"Of course, of course," Humph replied, though he didn't know one key signature from house key.

Mrs. Sidwell inhaled, then spread her arms, more like an eagle than a swan.

"Days are ending,
Birds are wending,
Back to the shelter of
Each little nest they love."

Her voice cracked on "love". It was a wholly unpleasant sound to Humph's ears and somehow devoid of any kind of recognizable loyalty to pitch.

Immediately, Mrs. Sidwell laughed and apologized.

"So very sorry. The day is young and I haven't even had my morning massage. I'm sure you understand."

An embarrassed silence followed. Finally Humph beckoned her to the couch.

"We'll have another go at that later, Mrs. Sidwell."

She was obviously happy to move on.

"Please call me Clarissa."

"Why thank you," said Humph.

After telling her that despite the cracked note, he said she was obviously passionate about theater.

Humph didn't know if it was possible to fake a blush but she appeared to do just that.

"Passion is what passion is," Mrs. Sidwell said.

The time was right, Humph decided. Time to move in for the kill.

"Have you known many performers, many actors? You must have gotten your passion and your theater savvy from somewhere, from someone?"

Mrs. Sidwell appeared to lose herself in thought. When she emerged, she almost blurted out a suggestion that a drink might be appropriate despite the relatively early hour.

"The arts teach us that we shouldn't hold back. All emotion is real. It's legitimate. It belongs on the table, evidence of our existence." As she made the statement, there was a defiant lift to her chin.

Humph was taken aback. What she said was profound. It didn't even sound like she was quoting someone. Was it possible she believed it? If so, she wasn't the looney he anticipated getting to know. She might be crazy but she wasn't an imbecile. She couldn't sing to save her life but why was she willing to be a laughingstock? By all appearances, she had done so repeatedly.

"So," she said softly, "what say you to a drink?"

Out of nowhere, the butler arrived. Was there a button hidden somewhere, one that rang for the help?

"Scotch," Humph said.

"And for you, madam, the usual?"

Mrs. Sidwell merely nodded, almost imperceptibly.

The drinks that were soon served on a silver platter were at least doubles by Humph's reckoning.

They were obviously the quantities the mistress of the household was expecting with her order for the of "the usual".

This was a woman in pain. A lunatic maybe, maybe not, but a woman in pain nevertheless.

"Forgive me," said Humph, "but someone hurt you, a lot, emotionally I mean."

"You're why I love people in *the business*, show business. You have hearts. My husband doesn't."

Humph maintained a stare. She didn't blink. Eventually, she said:

"I found love elsewhere. He was an actor, a beautiful boy, a black boy. He never told me to shut up. He never said to leave him alone. He always smiled when he saw me. He always wrapped me softly in his arms. No self-important macho pretensions."

Humph could barely contain his excitement.

"You say he was an actor. Was he on stage when you knew him?"

Mrs. Sidwell was rocking back and forth physically and emotionally.

"No. He was an understudy."

"What show, Mrs. Sidwell. One that I'd know?"

"Yes, you'd know it. *The Green Pastures*. He was the understudy of DeLawd, the main character. He could have been famous if he'd been given the chance to do just one performance. But you know what it's like, don't you."

Humph kept giving her time to sink into memories. Finally he said:

"How did he die?"

Mrs. Sidwell stared at Humph for the longest time.

Humph didn't blink, didn't budge. The silence grew oppressive.

"He betrayed me," said Mrs. Sidwell. I saw him with a girl, a black girl."

"What were they doing?"

"Nothing. Just talking. They both smiled a lot. I don't know why but I felt so jealous I wanted to die. Then…it's the craziest thing…I didn't want to die any more. I wanted to kill him. When the young girl went away, I walked up to him. He gave me that smile again. I almost vomited. Don't ask me to explain. Like a gentleman, he took me home and put me to bed. He lay down beside me, fully dressed. I pretended to sleep. A couple of hours later, I could tell by his breathing that he was asleep, too. I went to the kitchen and got a filleting knife. I was crying but I bent over him and slit his throat. I stopped crying as I watched life disappear from him. I never felt so cold inside. The next morning, I asked our butler to find some guys to take his body and dump it on a street somewhere, somewhere where lots of people get killed, a place where colored people get killed."

With all his willpower, Humph kept himself from opening his mouth. Let her talk. Don't close the spigot.

A minute later, Mrs. Sidwell half rose and thrust herself against Humph.

"Hold me! Hold me! Like a man!" She almost screamed the last words. Her acting was as melodramatic as her singing was off key.

Humph could only hold her and wonder how she could be so needy. She had everything, a rich husband and a life of luxury floating atop an ocean of economic despair.

He held her for at least 20 minutes until her sobs became wails and she had to sit up to breathe.

When her breathing returned to normal, Humph asked a question he never thought he would have a chance to ask today.

"Have you ever felt the need to kill another man?"

She screamed.

"Yes! Yes! Yes!"

The butler arrived.

It was clear this was not the first time his boss had become hysterical.

"I've called an ambulance, sir."

Half an hour later, the ambulance took her to Bellevue. The butler went with her and invited Humph to hop in as well. The butler rode with them to explain the need to take her in.

The butler appeared relieved that his boss was under psychiatric care as an inmate. Her husband had committed her for care before.

Humph and the butler left the hospital together. Humph suggested they have a meal or a drink somewhere, whatever the butler felt like. The butler nodded yes to Humph's suggestion that they pour a glass at Humph's place. The idea to get to know the butler a little better came from the fact that once his mistress had been admitted to hospital, he clearly relaxed and his words lost all pretension to advanced education. "Her husband is the real actor in the household." Humph decided there could be nothing worse than the butler's job.

CHAPTER 4

AFTER Humph poured two Scotches, his first question for the butler, whose name he had learned on their way to his place was Graham Lassiter, was whether he thought his mistress actually committed the murder and whether she was truly certifiable.

"You have your doubts?" Graham asked.

Humph said at the time of the hysterical confession, he believed her but now, having learned that her feet weren't solidly planted on the ground at the best of times, he was beginning to doubt the whole story.

"The affair part is true," said Graham. "I double as chauffer to her. Mr. Sidwell has his own chauffeur. I took her to assignations with the young actor, who, by the way, was as she described. He was young and handsome and genuinely sweet. She may have thought it was love but that was all in her mind. As for him, the attention of a wealthy, fabulously wealthy, white woman was too good to pass up. He was an immigrant from Haiti. From what I've read, that is very much a different world. My mistress bought him everything, from clothes to caviar."

Did Mr. Sidwell know of the affair?

"What is it they say in Westerns, Humph? Damn tootin' he knew. I think she went out of her way to rub it in. She would attend shows on the arm of the young actor. Over drinks with society people at intermission, she would leave the impression that he had won her approval as an actor, though in truth she'd only seen him rehearsing. To anyone who doubted their relationship, she made it known that she was now sponsoring his career. She would say things like, 'I've opened many a door for him with my producer friends.' Maybe she did. I don't know. The name Sidwell would open any door on Broadway."

"And…" said Humph.

"You mean to say, Humph, did it bother him much? I can't really say. I rarely saw him for more than a few minutes at a time. He left for work early in the morning and was almost never home for supper. The suppers between them that I witnessed, mostly they were quiet as a church with no service going on. Sometimes, as if bored by his steak, he'd say the dress she was wearing was 'unappealing, to say the least,' adding that he failed to understand how she could make such horrible fashion choices with all the money he had put at her disposal. Or he would say, 'Did you run out of make-up this evening?' He could be nasty, as nasty as anyone I've ever known. Where the hate came from, I haven't been around long enough to know.

"My mistress once told me she intentionally dressed down to annoy him. She even said, 'He's an ugly man in every way.'"

Humph said he was starting to get the picture, "the very sad picture."

"Forgive me," he added. "If she was going to kill

someone, why not her so-called husband?"

Graham didn't have an immediate answer. Humph liked him because he didn't spout things out that didn't bear scrutiny.

"As wobbly as her mental state was at times, she was smart enough to know how elevated their place was in society. A murder of someone like her husband would be investigated by every cop in New York. Politicians, particularly the ones whose election campaigns depended on his generosity, would scream for justice. And that would include our dear mayor, Johnny O'Brien. So, no. She wouldn't think of killing him for real. In her dreams, of course. For real, no."

And, added Humph, her position and her wealth and her influence, such as it was, depended on hubby dearest.

"That's sort of how I see it," Graham said. "But we can't rule out her wild moments. At one point, she was convinced Mr. Sidwell had hired an assassin to rub out her lover. How would she even find out about something like that?"

Humph poured another round. Humph changed his focus.

"What about you, Graham? What's your story? Something tells me you don't come from a long line of butlers."

Graham laughed.

"That obvious, is it?"

"I did one year of university, at Notre Dame. Got bounced out over a bogus claim that I harassed a good Catholic girl who taught at a nearby high school. We were lovers to be sure but her father didn't approve of me. I'm not sure why because, after all, I went to Notre Dame. You can't get more Catholic than that. Maybe it was because I didn't give a damn about football. He once asked me whether I'd met Knute Rockne. I answered, 'Who?' That's probably when he decided to charge me with assaulting his little girl."

Humph couldn't help but laugh. The story bolstered his disdain for organized religion.

The conversation between the two men veered toward everyday matters. Humph explained that Eve was battling to carve out a life on Broadway.

"I know a little bit about the obsession and the passion a goal like that requires," he said. "Her mother was a burlesque and vaudeville star, bless her soul."

Graham didn't say anything but he found it curious that a man with such disdain for religion asked that blessings be bestowed on someone he once knew. Maybe "bless her soul" was just an expression that slipped into everyday language without religious context. It just meant caring, loving.

Finally, Humph asked, "If you weren't a butler for a high-society household, what would you like to be?"

Graham got up from the wooden chair he'd been in for the past two hours and walked around the apartment. It was so small that his journey lasted about 10 seconds and his legs were as stiff as when he got up.

"How do you live in such a small place?"

"It keeps my mind from being distracted, if that makes any kind of sense," Humph replied.

"Maybe that makes a little sense. Not sure I could deal with it."

"OK, Graham, do you have an answer to my question? 'What would you like to be?'"

Graham spun around to face Humph directly and assertively declared:

"A choreographer. On Broadway, preferably. I have danced all my life, but privately as I'm sure you can understand. Indiana is not big on male choreographers or modern dancers. That's why I came to New York. To escape Indiana. If New York denied my dream, I vowed to make enough money to sail to France where artists are appreciated."

All the while Graham confessed to being a far different human being than circumstances suggested, Humph was thinking of Eve.

"Can I introduce you to someone who is trying to break down the same wall that Broadway insists you climb?"

"Of course, Humph, but I've been away from dance for so long working for rich lunatics, I'm far from ready to audition."

"No matter," said Humph.

"Connections are what matter. You need a foot in the door. My Eve might be able to arrange that. But hear me clearly, Graham, it's a one-shot deal. If you get an audition and have nothing to offer, your dream is history. New York doesn't wait on anybody."

Graham swore he understood. He said he needed months of practice. That was possible if Bellevue kept his mistress in custody for that long.

Humph didn't think that was likely. Sidwell would probably arrange to get her out for appearance's sake. It would also make her even more beholden to him.

Instead, Humph suggested that Graham immediately see Eve and request that she introduce him to someone who could complete his training as a dancer. It would have to be arranged immediately, before his mistress is released. Would you have the money for such lessons?"

To Humph's eyes, Graham was now an entirely different man than the one who greeted him at the door of Mrs. Sidwell's, the man who so carefully adjusted the brim of his new fedora. At that moment and throughout the interview with Clarissa, he was a helium-bloated pretender to the role of butler and protector of an even more bizarre pretender to citizenship in the stratosphere of New York's high society.

Graham paused, lost in thought.

"Yes, I'll come up with the money somehow."

He paused again.

"I've just had a crazy idea, one that's maybe not so crazy. My mistress so likes to believe she bathed in the lights of Broadway that maybe, maybe, maybe she would delight in the opportunity to single-handedly give me a hand up into that world, a financial hand up. Is that a crazy thought, Humph? I'm not at all embarrassed to suggest it because most of what we've been talking about for hours has been crazy."

Humph had been all set to tell Graham to be realistic about his present situation with Mrs. Sidwell fluttering every which way. If, by chance, she were to remain in Bellevue for an extended period of time, how secure would his employment be? Is it not possible that Mr. Sidwell would prefer to hire a butler less supportive of Mrs. Sidwell?

"You told me earlier that she liked the fact that when Mr. Sidwell questions you about her, you always reply, 'I think it best that you inquire of Mrs. Sidwell.'"

"Your present world," Humph added with the deepest voice his diaphragm could produce, "is more than precarious. If you want to pursue your dream, I would suggest you risk poverty and escape that madhouse."

After he said it, Humph wondered why he felt it necessary to be so, so, well, theatrical in delivering his advice. It was only sometime later that he formed the suspicion that he detested high-society phonies and didn't want to see an honest man like Graham tossed out someday like a dress that couldn't possibly be worn twice.

Graham remained silent for minutes. Humph refilled his glass.

When Graham left his thoughts, he looked Humph in the eye and drank the entirety of the new glass. He continued to look at Humph but his stare faded. In minutes, he lapsed into sleep. He was not a drinker.

Humph immediately called Eve.

"Rescue needed. Come now. No, I'm fine. Someone you should meet needs saving."

Eve was busy rehearsing herself. "It will be really late when I get there."

"That will be fine."

CHAPTER 5

LESS than an hour after calling Eve, Humph found himself drifting off like Graham. Aggressive banging on his door shook him awake. Angrily he pulled the door open. It was none other than the never-subtle ex-detective Duffy.

"Humph, my boy, evidence suggests that you've been imbibing. Care to offer a weary traveler a pick-me-up?"

Humph's annoyance vanished. Duffy was a rascal but there was no one better to work a case with.

"That Irish snout of yours is truer than any blood hound's nose. Scotch is on the menu."

"Thought so," said Duffy, triumphantly.

You could never tell how much Duffy had been drinking because his sober personality somehow still seemed to have been forged in a pub in the heart of Dublin. Who knows?

Maybe a publican babysat him as a lad. Duffy never spoke about his childhood.

As Duffy started to raise the glass Humph handed him, his detective's eye spotted a body slumped on Humph's bed, upper body on the mattress, feet on the floor.

Duffy turned to Humph, still holding his glass near his lips.

"Dead or alive?"

The instant after he matter-of-factly asked the question, he emptied his glass and parked himself on a kitchen chair. There were only two and Humph had squatted on the other one.

"Alive."

"That's refreshing. I'm off duty."

"You're always off-duty now, Duff," Humph exclaimed.

"Don't I know it, boyo. Man is not meant to sit on his laurels. They itch me arse, right through my britches."

"Do you ever go see the boys at the precinct?"

"I did at first but no one ever tells me about a case I would ever have wanted to sink my teeth into. Either the Depression has made New York as dull as friggin' Cleveland on a rainy Sunday, or my old brethren don't know what's really bubbling under the surface. You know as well as I, Humph, this big damn city is built on corruption, greed and a hell of a lot, what shall we say, of horniness."

"No disputing that, Duff," said Humph. "I still get work but nothing like our big case. My britches are chaffing, too, my friend. But enough melancholy. The Irish race would have controlled the world without that inclination to crying in your beer."

"I prefer to cry into a vessel of Scotch, if you don't mind."

Humph poured him another but left his own glass empty, wanting a clear head for Eve's visit.

"So, Humph, who's sleepin' in your bed?"

Humph gave Duffy the whole story, the murder of a Broadway actor, the confession of a high-society cuckoo, her bully of a husband, a Broadway pretender who sits on millions of greenbacks rather than laurels, and finally the only reliable participant in the story, a university-educated butler who really wants to become a Broadway choreographer.

"That's him, on the bed."

"Could you repeat all that, laddy?"

"You heard me, Duff."

"I thought life was supposed to be easier the older and the wiser we got, Humph."

"We all get older to be sure. But wiser? Not so sure about that."

Duffy nodded.

"True enough. But to the dogged go the rewards in copper heaven."

His smile was so big that Humph said he would love to work together again but he wasn't even sure what to investigate at the moment.

"Loose ends everywhere, Duff, and not a whisper of hard evidence."

Humph said Eve would join them soon, not to talk about the case but to talk to the butler, the guy on his bed.

"But the thing that keeps gnawing at me is that Eve, who is the one who first told me about this murder, said she had been told by someone in the know on Broadway that a woman did the dirty deed, and that the death slash of the murderer's knife was.... well, the guy's throat was delicately sliced, like maybe what a loving woman would do. That's why the rich lady's confession seemed to make sense at first."

"Have you talked to the woman who gave your girl that heads-up?"

"No. After giving me the news she ran away for some reason or another. Haven't seen her since."

"Well, Humph, tonight we'll give your Eve the third degree."

"No way in hell," Humph shouted.

Duffy grinned. Graham woke up. Eve knocked.

"I got it! I'm on Broadway. I got the role!" Eve was spinning like a Dervish just inside the door. "I am from now on only known as Felicia Montealgre." Eve mustered all the theatrical kitsch she could in delivering the line."

Eve rushed into Humph's arms. He felt her energy and spun her around several times, finally causing her feet to leave the floor.

"I did it, I did it, I did it! My name will be in *Playbill*."

Humph, proud as a father would be, kept hugging her.

It took Eve several minutes to realize they weren't alone.

"Duff," she said.

"Hi there, lass. You're a sight for sore eyes."

Her head turned to the young man sitting on the bed.

"I'm sorry to intrude, young lady. Humph invited me. My name is Graham."

Eve's "How do you do?" was said looking into Humph's eyes, not Graham's.

Humph lifted her up and sat her on the bed, next to Graham.

"Eve, let me explain."

He told her who Graham was, the butler of a woman who confessed to killing the actor. He also told her he had huge doubts that she was the killer.

"What I need to know, Eve, is who told you a woman was involved in the young man's death?"

Eve looked at the faces staring at her, then looked at Humph.

"Why, it was the woman who found his body. She's a make-up artist. She said the body smelled of perfume. The killer had to be a woman."

Duffy was the first one to break the long silence in the room.

"What do you know about this face-painting lady, the

make-upper you referred to? Does she work for your show, or another one? Why would she have found the body?"

Eve said that since her first talk with Humph she asked around. What she learned was that the apartment building where the young actor lived was owned by a consortium of Broadway producers who wanted to make sure their performers could find affordable accommodations in the Theater District.

"The rents are so reasonable that I'm thinking, now that I'm officially on Broadway, of applying. The make-up artist doesn't live there but... "

"But?" asked Duffy.

"This is so sad," said Eve. "She had a distant crush on the actor as well. They would have been such a cute couple."

"So where did the rich lady fit in?" Duffy asked.

Graham spoke up for the first time.

"Clarissa had a..."

"Who's this Clarissa lass?" asked Duff.

"Mrs. Sidwell, the producer's wife. She insists I call her Clarissa. I think it's because her husband shows her not the slightest affection. Though I'm a mere butler, using first names lets her think I'm a friend and confidant in her schemes."

"I like schemes," Duffy said, helping himself to another drink.

"First of all," Graham said, "I think she liked me initially because her husband didn't. However, she chose to ignore the fact that he liked no one to her knowledge. Her husband never addressed a word to me. As I told Humph, part of my job was to serve as a chauffeur to the family but Mr. Sidwell hired one for himself alone."

Graham said he believed Clarissa knew the affair with the young actor was something for show. It played into her larger fantasy of being seen by New York society as a mover and shaker in show business. It also played into her sincerely felt desire to embarrass her husband.

"Ergo," Graham concluded, "the beautiful young Haitian actor was worth every penny she spent on him, not just for drinks and suppers but luxury hotel suites for pretend assignations."

"What does Bergo mean?" Duff asked brusquely.

"No sir, not Bergo. The word was 'ergo'. It means, 'therefore'."

Duffy enjoyed riding roughshod over the King's English for the simple reason that the King of England was persona non grata where he came from.

Finally, Humph spoke.

"All this supports my theory that crazy Clarissa did not kill the actor. Why would she want to destroy her favorite toy? That fanciful relationship was her best way of boxing hubby's ears. You may not have noticed, but Clarissa cultivated our city's nastiest gossip columnists. She would pass on to them some cleverly constructed lie about her husband, putting him in a despicable light, and the columnist would simply write: 'We have this news on good authority. We ask you, dear reader, could it be true?' Damage done, mission accomplished.

"So no, killing the young man would serve no purpose. His death would have pricked her fanciful balloon and her life would have descended again into boredom and despair."

Eve stood again and faced the room. Humph wondered whether actors ever made speeches sitting down.

"OK, Humph. I'm starting to get your reasoning. But by confessing even though she's innocent, doesn't that make her nobody but a killer?"

"Absolutely," said Graham. "Even though my work for her was often humiliating, I now feel hugely sorry for her. Her story belongs in the hands of a skilled playwright."

Eve nodded her agreement, as did Humph."

Duffy blew his nose. When he put his handkerchief away he told Humph they had to visit to visit the make-upper lady.

"Can you help us locate her, Eve?"

"Of course. Can I come with you?"

"Absolutely not." The response to her question came simultaneously from Humph and Duffy.

"Don't you guys know that women today do all sorts of things they couldn't a decade ago. Right, Humph? My star example is you know who, Karena, a decorated NYPD officer."

Humph thrust open his arms in resignation.

Duffy raised his glass to her spirit.

CHAPTER 6

THE make-up artist lived on Avenue B between 10th and 9th Streets. The apartments there were modest but the entrance was handsome, the stairs perfect for settling in to view the parade of passersby on a hot evening.

As Humph stood on the stairs taking in the street, Duff leaned on the doorbell. A pretty young face pulled back the lace curtain to see who was calling. "Puerto Rican?" Duffy wondered. "Or Haitian?" He held up his old police badge. It was a criminal offence for him to do so now that he was retired. He was allowed to keep the badge as a souvenir. The door opened and Humph followed.

The girl said they should step inside because bad things might be about to take place across the street, in Tompkins Square Park.

"What do you mean?" Humph demanded.

"Come," she said. She was pretty and young, maybe late 20s at the most. Her voice was soft but commanding all the same. She led Duffy by his jacket sleeve to the window overlooking the park.

"Take your time. Maybe you'll understand and tell me what's happening."

While waiting for Duff to turn back to them, Humph asked: "Your name, it's Rebecca?"

"Yeah. How did you know?"

"Eve told me." Getting no response, he added that she was an actress and that she was his de facto daughter. "You have done her make-up." Humph described Eve in a little more detail, then added, "Eve told me you did make-up for *The Green Pastures* cast."

"Yes," the girl answered, still wary. Before Humph could reassure that he needed to clear up only a few details about the murder of a man who been an understudy for the show, Duffy looked back and said,

"For heaven's sake, Humph, you have eyes, too. Do as the lady said and look out the window. You're too damn old to be flirting with a maker-upper. Get over here."

Humph was enjoying the interaction. The exchange was the kind of thing he'd bring up in taverns months from now.

"So so tough, aren't you, Duff. Tell us about when that little sweet young girl took you by the ear and told you where to look for evidence."

Duff would curse him in ways Humph never imagined. In the end Humph would signal the barkeep to replenish the Irishman's glass.

"What's going on, Duff?"

"Coppers, scores of them, that's what's goin' on."

"Why?" Humph asked.

"Because I imagine that the mayor has ordered them to destroy the tents in the park. If they came just to sort out an isolated incident there wouldn't be so many of them.

They did the same thing two years ago. It was like a war. Homeless, starving people trying to push back coppers swinging billy clubs. There was blood everywhere and it wasn't the coppers' blood. At the time, I read that a thousand people lived here in the park. Why, in the name of all that's holy? I tell you Humph, no one, and I mean no one, the police chief, the mayor, the governor of the damn state ever, ever, ever said why!"

Humph noticed the young woman was crying.

"Talk to me," he said.

When Rebecca collected herself, she said quietly that she walked through the park every day.

"Sometimes they'd ask if I could spare anything, food or coins. You've never seen such desperation. Yet they were all soft-spoken and respectful. How many of them starved to death in those tents between the time I went to bed across the street and got up the next morning? Only God knows."

Humph took her hand into his and covered it with his other hand, so big that it disappeared. He let several minutes roll by.

"Truth time," said Humph, still softly hugging the young woman. "The reason we're here is that I'm a private investigator. I used to be a cop. My friend there, Duffy, he was a detective with the NYPD, one of the best I've ever known. He's retired now but when I work with him I feel I can solve anything. Which brings me to our reason for coming here. We need to know everything you know about the young actor's life and his death."

She looked everywhere but at Humph for at least a minute.

"What about those poor people?" Her voice had risen but the sound was raspy, ready to crack.

Humph reached for her hand again.

"My partner and I can't do much at the moment. I'm sorry." The word "sorry" hit such a low note that it seemed to jolt her awake, to the present, to the reality in her room.

Humph asked if she could forget for a moment the tragedy that was about to unfold in the park outside her window.

"*Es muy importante,*" he said. Those words all but exhausted his Spanish.

Rebecca looked him in the eye.

"*Hables?*"

"*No, lo siento.*"

"I can tell you things but they're just things. *Cosas.* They mean nothing to me."

"Maybe they will to me, or some other people who knew the young man," Humph said.

"One person for sure. Mrs. Sidwell. Did she kill him?"

"No, no, never. She worshipped him. I remember once at a party he looked hard at a young, beautiful woman and Mrs. Sidwell cried."

Rebecca waited for Humph to say something but he seemed flustered.

"I'm not very good at these women things, Rebecca. What did her tears mean?"

This time it was Rebecca who took a hand, Humph's mitt.

"She just wished deep down inside herself that a handsome young man looked at her that way. Even young women wish that. At her age, I bet she prayed that would happen, even if it didn't lead anywhere. We all want to be loved and respected. I know I do and I'm young compared to her. At her age, I think she felt she had to buy affection. I hope I never get to that point."

"Jesus Christ all mighty! Come here, Humph," Duffy demanded.

"My brothers, the fuckers, they're actin' like it's the Great War and they're charging enemy lines. Look, guns, batons, torches!"

Humph nudged him aside from the window and started digesting the scene.

Seconds later he could see the shape of the impending tragedy. Hundreds and hundreds of starving New Yorkers, unarmed and without enough food in their bellies to raise much resistance, about to be bowled over, kicked, beaten and dragged out of the park by his old comrades. He didn't know who gave the order to eliminate this Hooverville, the second largest in the city. In all likelihood it was the mayor. But why? Humph asked. This was America. The people being attacked, law-abiding Americans. Everyone—except the police or maybe just the mayor—knew they hadn't committed any crime except dire poverty.

This scene, thought Humph, was horrible enough. Did it mean that someday the city would try to pull the same stunt to magically eradicate poverty in Central Park? The Hooverville there was home to 8,000 people.

Humph returned to the sofa at Rebecca's side.

"So, you say you don't think Mrs. Sidwell killed the actor. Did you ever tell anyone, or even suggest to them that a woman killed the young man?"

Rebecca didn't answer. She stared at the floor.

"I'm asking you this because my girl Eve said you did. She's not a gossip."

During her silence, Duffy returned to the room and sat down in a chair facing the sofa.

Finally, Rebecca said, "I'm afraid."

"Of?" Humph said gently, hoping to spur her on.

"I'm really not sure but I think it was a woman from Haiti who killed him. I don't know her but Joel invited me out for a drink one night. There was nothing romantic, not that I would have minded. He was *muy bueno*. Really handsome. He regarded me as just another theater colleague. He said he could use some company. He was worried, he said."

"About what?" Humph asked. "Was he having trouble

getting another acting job?"

"That's what I was thinking at first but… You know he was Haitian, right?"

"No," said Humph. "I just assumed he was American."

"He was but he had family and friends from his homeland. What he told me the night we went out was that he was being followed. Sometimes he spotted a man in the shadows across the street. Sometimes it was a woman. They would stay nearby for too long to be a coincidence."

Rebecca then explained that they were Black and possibly Haitian. Joel said they suddenly appeared in his life after he joined a group of Haitian-New Yorkers at a demonstration in front of the office of Senator Robert F. Wagner.

"He said they were hoping that Wagner could influence the U.S. Marines stationed in Haiti to control the excesses of the country's dictator, Sténio Vincent."

She said that Joel bought her four glasses of rum to help her stay patient while listening to his long-winded explanation.

"He was obviously passionate about his heritage, which was sexy as can be, so I was happy to sip my rum and listen."

She said Joel explained that since taking power in 1930, Vincent ruled Haiti during a period of unprecedented peace. His followers in Haiti said it was his skill that had transformed the country. His opponents, especially those outside the country, said the peace was the result of oppression. They felt the silver-tongued president was setting himself up to become an outright dictator.

But thanks to the Marine presence, Joel had said, the U.S. controlled the country's purse strings.

"So who better than the Marines to clip Vincent's wings," he said. "After all, the Marines represented a democratic country. They should set a democratic example by preventing Vincent from illegally extending his stay in office. Haitians want democracy."

But in the end, the actor said, our hopes fell on deaf ears. "To our knowledge, Sen. Wagner never even raised our point of view in the Senate let alone fought for it."

"But," Rebecca said, "Joel was now sure he was a marked man for opposing this Vincent guy."

Rebecca's gaze slowly moved from Humph's face to Duffy's and back.

"I don't know but it's the only scenario that makes sense to me. Joel said that most of the time it was the woman following him and that's why I said that a woman killed him."

Humph gently squeezed her shoulder in appreciation of the admission.

"Why are you afraid?"

"What if they find out I talked about them to you? Joel told me they kill people here in American who oppose their president."

CHAPTER 7

ONCE home, Humph's first call was to his friend, Jerry Franklin, at the *New York World*.

"Do you know anything about Haitian murder squads in the city?"

"Thanks for saying, 'Hi, how are you, buddy,' crap like that."

"Sorry for the hundredth time. Repeat your question and give me time to answer. At this very moment, I am surrounded by three copy editors who think their questions are more important than some friend on the phone asking about where Haitians do their laundry. How about I call you back? You at home?"

By the time he called back, Duffy had arrived.

"This better be good," said Duffy the instant he walked in.

"Why?" asked Humph. "You not doing anything but sit on your fart box these days."

"A whiskey might encourage an agreement about that accusation."

Humph pointed behind him, to the counter topped by bottles.

"I hope you're not going to bore me with another lecture on the history of a country whose location I have no clue about. I merely assume it's too hot for human habitation."

"Pocket your ignorance for a minute, can't you?" Humph didn't rebuke his friend in anger. Duffy was proud of his ability to disguise his intelligence.

"It's possible that his Broadway murder has international origins."

"What the hell does 'international origins' mean?"

"It means that the murder of actor Joel Jean-Baptiste was committed by a Haitian representing the prime minister of said country, the kind you love, hot, humid, sultry. The kind of place where you can drink a quart of whiskey and sweat it out by noon the next day."

"But, sir Humph, what is the connection? The bloke was murdered in Chelsea."

"Bloke? To my knowledge, you boggers don't say bloke. We Yanks don't say bloke. And no one has ever referred to a Haitian as a bloke. Have you been retired for mere misconduct or is the real reason senility?"

Franklin phoned back to say his shift at the paper was all but over.

"I talked to a couple of reporters and we came up with a few clippings that might at least give you a little background about Haitian attitudes towards the U.S. of A. For a small drink, I'd be willing to drop by and give you a bit of a run down. Sound good?"

"It sounds good," said Humph, "but first let make sure Duffy hasn't downed my supply."

Duffy immediately pointed toward himself and mouthed "Who, me?"

"There's a drop or two left. See you soon, Jerry."

He turned back to Duffy.

"Rebecca's thought that it was a woman who killed the actor makes sense even though a man was also following him. A woman, especially a Haitian woman if she was pretty, could get close to the young man more easily than a man. A knife cut across his throat somehow seems more a female gesture, you know, instead of a gun or a hammer blow to the noggin."

"You've got my vote on that," said Duffy, toying with his empty glass.

Humph enjoyed the torture, making Duffy wait until the newspaperman arrived. Unfortunately, he arrived just a few minutes later.

"Got a lift from a buddy at the paper," Jerry explained.

Humph offered him a small wooden chair at the rickety table or a place on his bed next to Duffy.

Once he had his drink, and Duffy had his, the Irishman stared him in the eye and said, "Laddie, start by telling me where the fuck Haiti is. Can you do that for me?"

Jerry glanced at Humph, surprised. Humph nodded.

"Well, Duffy, I'm sure you know the thrilling story of Teddy Roosevelt leading his Rough Riders up San Juan Hill in Cuba during a little affair known as the Spanish American Civil War. Made Teddy an American hero. Now, picture yourself at the south-eastern tip of Cuba. You get drunk as can be under the blazing Cuban sun and you decide to go for a long swim, a very long swim. You plunk your empty glass in the sand and jump into the welcoming waters of the Caribbean. You head due south. Being the he-manly Irishman you are, your stroke is strong and before you know it Cuba has disappeared from view. Unbeknownst to you, the current gently tugs you a tad south-eastward. Enjoying the warm water, you drift off. You doze afloat. Suddenly, you're awakened by exploding surf. The waves carry you, propelling you toward palm trees and distant mountains. You stagger ashore. You are in Haiti, Duffy, in the north. You've covered a great distance, but, after all, you're Irish."

Humph almost fell off his chair he was laughing so loud. Duff glowered at both of them and helped himself to another drink.

"So, Jerry..." Humph stood up. He didn't have to say the words, "It's time to get serious."

"Yeah," said Jerry, handing him the few clippings he'd been able to find. "The story on top is about the demonstration staged by your dead friend and other Haitians urging the government to put the Haitian prime minister in his place. They'd appealed directly to a New York senator, none other than our dear, beloved defender of human rights, the Prussian-born Robert F. Wagner. The Haitians had figured the human rights of Haitians would be right up his alley. But the demonstration, which was small to begin with, fizzled. There's no record of the senator even raising the subject on the Hill. Wagner would have known that none of the demonstrators had become naturalized citizens yet, which meant they couldn't vote."

Humph interrupted. "Why does the clipping say at the top, *New York World Telegram*? I though the *Telegram* was another paper."

"High-finance," answered Jerry. "We've merged. Better get your press card updated, Humph."

The newspaperman went on to explain that a tiny, seemingly harmless demonstration, by rights, should not have upset anyone in the Haitian community, here or in Haiti. The Haitians in New York.... there are more than a few...they haven't caused the slightest bit of grief here. To my knowledge, unlike their homeland, there are no Haitian gangs here in the city. On the surface, the idea of a Haitian killing your young Haitian actor is a huge stretch."

Jerry paused and shuffled through the clippings.

"What is less obvious about them is, like Haitians back in Haiti, American Haitians want the U.S. to clear out of the country once and for all. To a man, they feel passionate about that. We took control of the country in 1915 following the assassination of their president and hundreds of others by Dominicans."

He turned to face Duffy.

"The Dominican Republic is next door to Haiti. The two countries hate each other although thousands of Haitians work there. Haitians are all originally from Africa, brought there as slaves. Dominicans think they're still Spanish, even the blacks, and therefore superior. Makes our American brand of racism almost seem mild in comparison."

After a moment, he continued exploring the clippings:

"Still on a racist note, there was a big flap in 1930 when a member of the commission here in the U.S. that oversees our presence in Haiti, had the temerity to raise the fingers of an elderly Haitian woman to his lips and gently kiss them. He said he did so out of gratitude because the old woman thanked him, and the U.S., for having delivered them from the violence of the outlaws who controlled so much of the country. The idea of a white American kissing the fingers of a black Haitian enraged people across America."

Jerry explained that in certain regards the U.S. was not hated, and in the young actor's case, they felt the U.S. could still help them.

"But if you look at editorials in a great many newspapers, we regarded Haiti as pain in the neck, one that we should say goodbye to. We didn't really give a damn about them. The commission tried to tell us we brought Haitians freedom. Truth is, we didn't. Haitians know that.

"So your boy's approach, to ask us to tame their prime minister, was simply a pragmatic one. It didn't mean he wanted us to stay in control of his country."

Duff cleared his throat.

"Young man, I sincerely feel elucidated. My world has become a tad larger. I mean that. You should become a writer or something."

Jerry didn't know how to respond. Humph came to the rescue.

"As contradictory as it was, Duffy's response was a backhanded compliment. Most people regard that as a good moment to quit his company. You're most welcome to stay and discuss this case. I'm just saying that Duffy is Duffy."

Jerry smiled. "I'll stay if you don't mind."

"Where can I go to meet Haitians here?" asked Humph.

"Many are scattered throughout Manhattan but I think most live in Harlem. There are a lot of other people from the Caribbean there and there's a lot of music they'd be comfortable with. Probably food, too, I'd guess."

Humph then asked him, "Do you have any Haitians of your staff at the paper?"

Jerry was taken aback by the question. Finally he admitted,

"We have no Haitians on staff. We have no Blacks on staff. It's not a rule but they don't approach us and we don't go looking for them."

"Any Latinos?" asked Humph.

"Sorry, but the answer's the same."

They all sat silent for a while until Humph stood and said, "Everyone out. I've got a long day of hoofing tomorrow."

CHAPTER 8

BEFORE setting out on his journey to Harlem, Humph
went to Rebecca's apartment on Avenue B. Maybe she had
remembered something else, or simply had a new theory.
Never had Humph faced a more bewildering case. Fact: a
young man with a slit throat. Suspects: none yet several.
Evidence: zilch.

"Let me get dressed," she said upon answering the door.
"I have to go to work this morning."

That was not what Humph wanted to hear. However he
told himself to be patient.

When Rebecca returned to the tiny living room, she
was resplendent in an emerald-green gown.

"Are you going to a party at this hour?"

Rebecca laughed.

"No, I'm going on a movie set. I will be doing make-up as usual but they want me to act. It's an odd movie. It's called Charlie Chan something or other. He's a Chinese detective of great fame, according to the studio's description of the story. I met him when I auditioned. You know what, Humph, he's American. Not an ounce of Chinese blood in him. And the strangest thing is that while they wanted me to act some silly little role, as an African spy or something like that, they insisted that I do Charlie Chan's make-up, which is mainly giving him slanted eyes. It took me more than an hour. In the end, I didn't think he looked Asian at all but the movie director was happy."

How racist was America? Humph had never travelled outside of New York City so he couldn't answer that question from experience. But he knew the city was already being talked of as some sort of melting pot. Land at Ellis Island as a foreigner, then take a short ferry ride to the city and step ashore as a supposed American. What a myth, thought Humph. He knew the hatred these naïve immigrants would face.

He told Rebecca why he wanted her company. She listened without expression when he said he needed her company today because she wasn't white.

Her response was a long time coming.

"You know, Humph, I understand why you're asking me this. I think you're a decent guy, for a white man. But do you know what it feels like to constantly be reminded that you're not white, as if that's something I want to be? It's not something you dismiss automatically for some supposed greater cause. Why didn't you just ask for my help without the racial context?"

Humph reached behind him and felt a chair. He slumped into it. He couldn't look at Rebecca right away. He thought of his parents who despised any kind of intolerance, especially here in American where mankind was welcome. They were Jews. They knew everything about racism. They didn't raise Humph as a Jew or anything else.

That was their new faith. Not Jewish, not Black, not Asian, not anything except a human being.

"What," his father exclaimed more than once, "what was simpler?"

When Humph collected his thoughts, he realized this was not the time to proclaim his non-bias and its origins.

Crestfallen, Humph stood.

"I'm so sorry," he said.

He was at the door when Rebecca stopped him.

"If you want to talk about this later we can. In the meantime, I want to help you because that beautiful boy didn't deserve to die. What is it that you want me to do?"

"In simple terms, I want to find a Haitian who has heard of the secret police from Haiti that operates here and where I might track them down. Secondly, I want to find someone who could verify that our dead actor was apparently dating a wealthy, white society woman."

"That won't be easy," Rebecca answered. "Black immigrants here toe the line. They don't want to raise any interest on the part of law enforcement. Just like home-bred American gangsters they'll likely give us their equivalent of 'Don't know nothin' about that or anythin' else, copper.'"

After a moment, she added:

"Haitians go to movies, too. I can hear it now," said Rebecca with a smile that stopped Humph in his tracks, "Cagney with a Haitian accent."

After digesting her ideas, Humph asked if she would have time to go prowling in Harlem and other places tomorrow.

"I think so," she said, stepping carefully into a taxi to avoid damaging her elegant green gown. The cab would take her to the set of the latest Charlie Chan movie.

Though it was only morning, Humph decided to call it a day. On his way home, he stopped by Eve's apartment. Nobody home. He'd forgotten that she'd finally landed a role on Broadway. God knows what time she would be finishing rehearsing. As a substitute for her conversation, he bought a copy of *Daily Variety Gotham*, whose coverage of entertainment focused on New York City, not Hollywood. When he got home he kicked off his shoes and opened the paper. He started at the back and worked toward the front.

Humph finally reached Page One. There, in screaming large type, were the words:

"2nd B'way Actor Bites Dust."

"Details are scant at press time," the story said, "however what is known is that the actor, whose name police have not divulged, had been involved in some sort of sordid ménage-à-trois."

It went on to speculate that:

"The debonair understudy in the cast of the Pulitzer Prize-winning show *The Green Pastures*, who was stabbed to death recently, apparently by a woman, was also involved with a woman from this city's high society.

"Can we dare speculate that high-society women in our fair city are using, abusing, then disposing of handsome young actors? Premature, perhaps. We'll find out."

Humph threw the paper on the table so forcefully that it flew to the floor on the other side. He'd seen the gawdy masthead before but never read a copy. Humph still proudly possessed his press credentials from the 1927 investigation he broke. He respected journalism but not wild imaginations and invitations to no more than titillation for profit.

When he calmed down, he had to admit that New York was a bizarre beast of a city. Without rampant rumor and nearly libelous gossip, would the city be like a drunk deprived of his next drink?

Tomorrow, he'd call Jerry. Afterwards, he hoped to see Eve about the current case and the new one, if it was real.

CHAPTER 9

HUMPH got up bright and early. Curiosity got the best of him. He needed to know more about the murder of Actor No. 2, as he catalogued it in his head.

A few blocks from his apartment, he grabbed a copy of the *Daily News*. The murder was real. It dominated the paper's front page.

He realized he was starved for more than news about the murder. He couldn't remember having eaten a bite the day before. He needed a New York breakfast.

Hashbrowns, sausage, eggs, and enough toast to erect a high-rise on his table.

He squeezed his bulk onto the seat of a table at a diner on East Broadway. He read the lead story. It mentioned that the actor had been frequently seen with a bejeweled woman at theater events and minor society events. His handsome smile and lack of opinions made him acceptable. The woman bore the Vanderbilt name but the paper's morgue had been unable to confirm a connection with Vanderbilt royalty, American style. Thus far, she had refused to speak to the press or police. One thing she did admit to was having a flying squad of lawyers to do her talking on any matter, big or small.

The paper had dug hard overnight for facts. They learned which events she was seen at with a young, handsome man, whom they assumed was the dead actor. They talked to people who had attended those events and even found photos of the two on the table of a woman who claimed to be an intimate friend of the esteemed Miss Vanderbilt. Under questioning, she admitted that her esteemed friend had been married to someone in the Vanderbilt family but had divorced. As soon as the divorce decree was final, she had started legal proceedings to legally change her maiden name to Vanderbilt.

Humph reread the story. Something about it rang untrue but he couldn't put his finger on it beyond the bizarre name change. She was a Vanderbilt in marriage. "Once a Vanderbilt, always a Vanderbilt." Was that her belief?

Questions were racing around Humph's mind, multiplying by the minute. Finally, he snapped to. One thing at a time. Next up, once he'd digested breakfast, was Rebecca. Humph was too full to immediately squeeze himself out from behind the table but he did manage to find the strength to cross his fingers that she would come to his aid today. A silly thought, he knew, but he was dying to ask her what Charlie Chan would do now to unearth Joel Jean-Baptiste's murderers.

After a second cup of coffee, Humph relaunched himself. Outside the restaurant, he debated going to Harlem on his own in search of Haitians who might or might not know anything about Joel's murder or returning home to wait for a possible call from Rebecca. He decided in favor of Rebecca. Though it was still morning, the day was already becoming hot. Gumshoe work was exhausting on such days. Since he had no leads, he'd be searching blind. Miles of unneeded steps. He knew from experience that unlike Manhattan, Harlem had managed to maintain some hills, tough on coppers and PIs and cartage horses, agreeable to the eye for everyone else. When Manhattan's mathematically precise street grid was created for Midtown and above in the previous century, the city declared war on its rolling hills and trees.

Humph liked living downtown where streets dared to curve and refused to go due south or due north. Human nature wandered all over the place and streets should, too, Humph figured.

Though hot, the late-spring sunshine was pleasant as he walked toward Henry Street. If it weren't for the Great Depression that had swallowed up uncountable New Yorkers, this spring could have been seen as a bright new beginning for the city and America. Just three months ago, in February, Prohibition had been struck down by Congress after a draconian 16 years. Like almost every American, Congress was in dire need of revenue. Prohibition had turned off that tap. Now, taxes on the sale of booze would fill its coffers instead of those of gangsters. The people would still be poor but they would no longer have to pay fines for having been caught buying alcohol.

By the time Humph got back to his place, he was happy to sit. It always seemed to him that as the humidity rose outside, his weight, already substantial, followed suit. He fought the urge to take off his shoes because that might encourage sleep. He moved his chair closer to the phone just in case he nodded off anyway.

When the ring ambushed him an hour and a half later, it was Eve on the line. She wasn't sure why but rehearsals for Sunday had been suspended. Today was Friday.

"I can't remember my last day off," she said. "I'd like to spend it with my leading man."

Humph still had a foot in sleep-deprived dopiness. "Who, pray tell, would that be?"

"Silly," Eve exclaimed. "You. You're my leading man."

"Silly me is right, my dear. I promise to stay home Sunday. Give me a call before you start heading my way. Anything special you want to eat?"

"I never know ahead of time. Let's hit the diner across the street."

"Deal."

Humph had no patience for cooking anyway.

Humph needed a dose of Eve more often than he cared to admit. For the rest of the day he felt mellow, his usual state of restlessness having evaporated. Was it because Eve made him remember her mother, his great love? Humph didn't literally picture Sonny too often but he couldn't escape the feeling that she was somehow always there with him. He had admitted that to Eve because she was her daughter and she had a right to know her mother still lived in him somehow. Humph never admitted that to anyone else, not even Duffy, his longtime copper buddy. He'd probably assert that some ancient Celtic devil-babblin' fairies were at work on him.

Humph decided to give up on the day and lie in bed with a book. It was too hot for pajamas. He hoped nightfall would bring him relief. There was no fire escape for him to sleep on and the last time he went to the building's roof he was greeted by a carpet of squirrel excrement enabled by an elm tree that somehow escaped execution. It sat in the alley behind the Henry Street tenements, an alley that was too narrow for a horse and carriage to pass through it. The tree reached high above the four-story building Humph inhabited, as if reaching for the sunlight. Squirrels had discovered it long ago and learned they could easily leap to the roof and back to the tree's branches. Few people climbed to the roof. The super was too old and fat to even contemplate the idea. Humph found the little buggers kind of cute when he sat eating peanuts in a park, reading his newspaper. But they were anything but here in their field of shit.

Thousands of New Yorkers slept on fire escapes and rooftops in summer. It was rarely comfortable but it made way for a necessity in life: breathing.

The book Humph chose was one he got the previous week from the nearby library. The librarian was at least 50 years old but she was more than merely adept at flirting with him and honoring the "silence please" ordinance. She was a shark in Humph's mind. He had to admit that he enjoyed the duel. The book he chose was *Brave New World*, by Aldous Huxley. "Came out last year," the librarian said. She batted her eyes and added, "You're quite the intellectual, aren't you, deary."

Humph held his laughter until he stepped down onto Grand Street. Her performance always reminded him of silly vaudeville acts he'd seen years ago before the rise of real theater on Broadway.

As he lay back in bed with his book, remembering the amorous librarian, Humph felt a wave of affection for mankind, which was not common in his profession. The more quirks and idiosyncrasies the better. The brave new world that Huxley envisioned was that of a new generation of stupefied and stunted individuals, devoid of emotions, mindlessly devoted to the state. After a couple of chapters, he laid the book on his lap and stared at the ceiling. He felt a shiver for an instant, the moment he saw America trying to impose the same vacuous hell on Americans. "There is one church. There is one color. There is one language. All others are wrong and will be eliminated." Those words weren't in the book but the book gave birth to them in Humph's mind. Was that not what the morality that underlay Prohibition represented, or the resentment toward the immigrants the Statue of Liberty welcomed?

Humph finally returned to the book. It intrigued him but he knew reading it was leaving him depressed. It was too real.

When he woke up the next morning, the book was on the floor, open. When he picked it up, he hoped it would reveal the last page he read, but no. The pages must have taken on a life of their own when they were flung from the bed.

Though he hadn't had a drop of whiskey, he felt hungover. Was that the downside of too much thinking? Or was it too much dreaming? Humph sensed he was still in full combat mode. His dreams were still assaulting him. He wasn't a believer in dreams. It was as if he was facing an attack from a part of himself he didn't recognize. He didn't know how to fight it. Then a moment of clarity. His own voice was telling him to put on the coffee. He obeyed immediately, then sat motionless. He saw his clothes on the floor but they seemed miles away.

Minutes later, just as he rose to take the percolating coffee off the stove, there was a knock at his door. Not entirely free of the mental swamp, he had a moment of paralyzing panic. Finally, sanity prevailed. He took the coffee off the stove and threw himself across the bed to get his pants. As he pulled them on and grabbed his shirt, he called out:

"Be right there, Eve." He'd forgotten she planned to visit Sunday, not Saturday.

The knocking stopped.

CHAPTER 10

HUMPH opened the door and instantly stepped back.

It took a few seconds but it seemed like forever. He was looking at Rebecca. Her face registered the alarm that would beset anyone looking at a giant madman.

"What brings you here, Rebecca? I mean, you're welcome, of course, but I didn't expect you so soon."

He poured a coffee and set it before her, returning to the counter to pour himself one. Over his shoulder, he asked about the city's attack on the homeless encampment at Tompkins Square Park.

"Everything went silent about 30 minutes after you left me," Rebecca said. "I didn't dare cross the street to see what the police had done. I thought there might be some cops who stayed behind and they might think I was one of their targets, the bastards."

Though she was angry when Humph and Duffy visited her at her place the night of the police action, and she was clearly still upset, Humph noticed that her voice never rose much in pitch or volume. However, her eyes betrayed the anger.

"I got a call from an actress last night. She was playing in *Conquest*. It was shut down after just 10 shows. She said another Broadway actor had been murdered. Not from her show but a guy she knows."

Humph stared at her for a moment, then raised three fingers, the new toll of murdered actors.

Rebecca nodded. "What's going on?"

"I don't have a clue," Humph said. "Do you have any details about this third murder?"

"None, except it happened two nights ago at a restaurant somewhere on the Upper West Side."

"Sit tight, Rebecca. I'm going to run out to get the morning papers."

When Humph returned, Rebecca was lying on his bed.

Humph threw the papers on the kitchen table.

Rebecca sat up.

"This is almost too much, Mr. Humph. Broadway is the most beautiful place in the world to work. I've never ever heard of violence of any kind. I've never even heard of somebody's wallet being stolen. Everyone is too busy building dreams for themselves and creating dreams for the people who buy the tickets."

Humph listened and thought about what she said.

"Surely people get jealous of the success of others, the roles they get. Actors are human, after all, even on Broadway."

Rebecca shrugged.

"I guess. I just haven't seen it. People get into spats, yes, but murder?"

"And, in fairness to your Broadway colleagues, the first two murders were apparently committed by outsiders, one by Haitian nationalists, the other by a cuckoo rich dame."

Rebecca, large eyed, nodded.

"Let's start going through the papers," Humph said, moving to the table and putting one at Rebecca's place.

Ten minutes later it was Rebecca who found a mention.

The headline was: "Chelsea Diners Lose Appetite When Murder Lands on Menu."

She handed the paper to Humph. It was the *Daily Mirror.* His index finger moved down the column faster than anyone could read, thought Rebecca.

"The actors and a male companion had just started eating when a middle-aged woman wearing a black gown suddenly stopped at their table, lifted a revolver from her large white purse and fired two quick shots, one hitting the actor in the chest, the other in the head."

"Another woman," said Humph. "The story says she calmly pointed the gun toward diners and staff as she backed her way to the front door, somehow disappearing in no time at all, according to people who ran after her onto the street."

Humph said he thought she sounded like a professional assassin.

"But why?" Rebecca demanded.

Humph returned to the two papers he'd been going through, turning the pages almost frantically. Nothing in one of the papers. In the *Journal American,* a short story.

"It says something very, very interesting. Something we haven't thought about. The dead actor performed in a show that was financed mostly by a man named Jacob L. Burley. According to the story, the second dead actor was to perform in a show scheduled to hit Broadway in the fall. It too is produced by Burley."

Looking at Rebecca, Humph wondered out loud whether these murderous women were being paid by enemies of Burley, whoever he was.

"But how on earth would a Haitian hit squad be involved in the first murder, the one the crazy high-society lady is involved in?"

"Your guess is as good as mine at this point," said Humph.

When Rebecca turned down the offer of another coffee, Humph asked if she would accompany him to Harlem to search out Haitians who might know something.

"Why bother now? Do you really think Joel's murder is separate from the other two? I mean, there's a connection between two of them, the producer, but…"

"But," interrupted Humph, "we can't rule anything out. Do you know who produced *The Green Pastures*? Whose money was behind it?"

She saw his point.

"Ask my Eve, or crazy Duff. I'm a relentless plodder. Don't have the brains to handle two ideas at once. I sleep better mowing down theories one by one, if that makes any sense to you."

"You know what I would do, Mr. Humph?"

"You'd ask Charlie Chan?"

That stopped Rebecca in her tracks. She slapped Humph on the knee. The joke elicited her first smile.

"What I would do," she continued, "would be first find out about this producer guy, the big money guy. The Haitians in Harlem today will still be there later."

Humph liked her logic, and he loved the way she didn't feel obliged to agree with him. It was a lot like Karena. Young women today were definitely a new breed.

"So, now that that you are chief detective, where do we start? I'm trusting that your Broadway experience might offer some slightly open doors as a starting point."

"I'll have to think about that," Rebecca replied with a smile. The big man wasn't as scary as she thought.

CHAPTER 11

AS planned, Eve arrived just before noon the following day. The flat offered little free space but she managed to wedge in a pirouette as she hummed *Give My Regards to Broadway*. She landed gracefully in one of Humph's delicate old chairs at the kitchen table.

She was beaming.

"At last, Eve, you're one of *them*."

"Your non-committal face gives me no clue as to whether your 'them' are good buys or bad."

"Good, more than good," Humph exclaimed, accepting that he can be hard to read now and then. Eve had often told him that. "The citizens of Broadway. Who else would I be talking about?"

Eve stopped teasing him and stood to accept his congratulatory embrace.

"I'm so thrilled. I'm proud of you."

"Not half as thrilled as I am," Eve added.

"Details, my dear. Details. The interrogation has begun."

"May the accused women have a drink first?"

"Thought you'd never ask."

As he handed her the drink, he said: "Your mom would be so, so proud that you're still following in her footsteps."

Eve nodded her agreement. No words were necessary.

"OK, young lady," resumed Humph. "Should you want another drink later, well that depends on the answers you provide right now. What's the show called?"

"It's a musical called *The Road Back Home*. My stage name is Jenny.

"What's the setting, what's the story?"

"It's about a young gaggle of singers and dancers who've been on the road since the Crash of 1929. We left New York shortly after. We figured the veterans of Broadway would devour the few remaining jobs as ticket sales plummeted because no one has any money. After three years in nameless towns, cheap, stinking motels and theaters that were really school auditoriums, and shows that nobody—nobody— bought a ticket to, we made a pact to do the impossible, to stick together until we could sing, dance and act our way back to the bright lights of Broadway."

"I'm sold. I'll pay to see that."

"I am mostly a hoofer but I have a duet to sing with our road manager, who dreams of making it to Broadway, too."

"You've earned a second glass," Humph said.

As he put it down on the table in front of her, Eve drained the first glass, which he deposited in the sink.

"When can I see the show?"

"We're supposed to open in early December. There's an eternity of rehearsals in between. Everything is done over and over and over again. You might get the steps perfect in two tries but if you land a little too slow in the third the choreographer bellows, 'One more time.' Eventually, some of us get hungry and we glare at people who mess it up and keep us on stage."

"Heaven forbid, Eve, but have you ever deprived your colleagues of food?"

"I thought you were on my side. Geez."

After a moment, she added: "I accept bribes to not mess things up. Pay up, girls and boys, and everyone eats on time."

"You don't do that, do you?" Humph's alarm was sincere.

"No, of course not. But I used to have to deal with that crap when I was stripping. The club managers wouldn't know the difference between a pas-de-deux and paws-off. If they thought your performance was half-hearted and not sexy enough, they'd get in your face and try to get into whatever else they thought they could. I kept my nails long and drank lots of milk to keep them strong."

"Glad to hear it," said Humph.

"Broadway's a breeze compared to clubs."

"How can you keep working on the same number for the next five months?"

Eve explained that the dancers had not just one number to perfect but 11 numbers.

"And it's still a work in progress. You keep hearing they're going to work in a new number. The actors get it just as bad. Script changes every other day."

"Do you go home fuming?"

"Are you kidding? I've never had more fun getting pissed off."

"Lunch," Humph said with a smile.

"Lunch."

"You're worse than a damn director," Eve added as she moved to the door.

As agreed upon, they crossed the street to a diner.

"You deserve a classier place than this for a celebration

of your arrival on Broadway."

"You know me better than that, Dad. The happiest part of my new job is stopping at the hot dog cart on 45th. The vendor has gotten to know me. He calls me Miss Sauerkraut."

Young people can be so incredibly alive, thought Humph as he dug into his pork chops and mashed with gravy. Eve chose a liver steak buried in green peas.

When they returned to Humph's place, he told her he had some questions to ask.

"Just speculation. Based on very little. Maybe just based on the fact that we have no viable leads in three murders, all Broadway actors. Until now, there has never been a murder of a Broadway actor. Not one. Now we have three in less than a month."

"I only heard of one, that Haitian fellow, the one who was an understudy for the lead in *The Green Pastures*. I don't think he ever got a chance to fill in. It can't be connected to Broadway, right?"

Humph looked at his feet before answering.

He decided to simply summarize the three murders.

"We think a crazy society woman killed the first one, the young Haitian man. We think they were lovers. We know he saw other women, as befitted his youth, but we think she was obsessed with him. He understood that and was happy to be a kept man, one who was accompanied by a high-society white woman to the city's highest circles. We think such a romance, or the appearance of a romance, was her way of embarrassing her husband, a frigid, arrogant financier who openly had other women on his arm at gatherings where their small world would have expected to see his wife.

"Her romance with a young, exceedingly handsome Haitian actor, got her into the gossip columns. She had little else to make her happy. She lived in a palatial apartment on Fifth Avenue, a place her supposed husband rarely visited.

Servants made sure she never had to do anything. That drove her insane."

Eve asked how the young man was murdered.

"His throat was slit. The city medical examiner said it was done gently, with a small exceedingly sharp blade. He said it was as if the victim was asleep at the time. The wound was so cleverly done, he would not have been awakened. He would have simply bled out in his sleep."

Humph then explained that the woman claimed no recollection of the event. She was clearly traumatized by the young man's death.

"She was scatter-brained, to be polite about it. I can believe she engineered the fake romance. All it took was money and her access to the people who count in his world, producers, agents, other stars. But I just can't believe she had the character to be able to climb on top of him in his sleep, raise his head and put the knife in a position to slit his throat."

Her husband, by all accounts a bastard, hastily signed the approval needed to commit her to Bellevue.

"She's still there. As for the second murder, a well-dressed woman walked into a restaurant in Chelsea where a handsome young actor was dining with two friends, one of them an attractive young woman. This time, the end came when the well-heeled woman pulled out a pistol and shot him between the eyes and calmly walked out."

"And the third?" asked Eve.

"Let's just say that dining is not good for your health. Another well-dressed woman pulled a gun on a handsome actor. I don't have any more details. It just happened."

"My God," said Eve, incredulous. Having once been kidnapped by bootlegging gangsters and rented out as a prostitute, she was no stranger to the city's dark side. "I know I just started on Broadway but this is too close for comfort."

Humph then asked if the name Jacob L. Burley meant anything to her.

Eve sipped her drink and thought.

"No, don't think so. Is he an actor?"

"No," said Humph. "He's some kind of money guy. Apparently he has financed one show that's now being produced and may have money in a second. Not that there's any evidence right now, but these killings have been so professional in a way that there is a possibility at least two of them, if not all three, were paid-for assassinations meant to undermine the shows Burley is producing. However, we know nothing of Burley at the moment. That's our next task."

"Our task? I don't have time to investigate, Humph."

Quickly he explained that he was investigating with Eve's make-up friend, Rebecca.

"She came to see me the other day," said Humph.

Eve grinned. "Do I smell romance in the air?"

"Nonsense. It's just that she's a Broadway insider. I don't know my way around in your world, so I need her help."

"Sure, sure," said Eve, still grinning. "She's good looking, isn't she."

"Eve, what the hell does that have to do with anything."

Eve had won. Her Humph was flustered.

Eve then earned a third drink by offering to ask around about money people on Broadway.

When Eve left just before supper time, Humph realized that he needed to get to Duffy and wind him up enough to make him pursue the possibility of mob money being behind Broadway shows. Duffy detested being without a case to pursue. He was acquainted with the first murder of an actor but that seemed, as he put it the night Jerry Franklin from the *New York World* was there, a cut-and-dried case of 'bonkers society broad forgets her manners and kills a guy. Case dismissed.'

When Eve vanished down the steps, Humph dialed Duffy's number.

"I need to talk to you. Are you planning on being hungover tomorrow morning or can I visit you, say 9?'

"Let me check my schedule, little man. Let's see, let's see. The odds in favor of sobriety at this very moment are 5-3. Can't be more specific than that."

Humph knew a good thing when he heard it.

"Make sure you know where your thinking cap is by the time I arrive."

CHAPTER 12

HUMPH handed Duffy a sweet roll at the door to his apartment. Then, as Duffy stared at him, Humph unbuttoned his jacket and revealed what Duffy thought would be a pistol. Instead, in Humph's holster, was a small bottle of bourbon."

"You may enter," said Duff. He sounded sober.

Once inside, Humph handed him the bottle.

"Bourbon! What's got into that brain of yours? Is it situated so far above the floor that you don't get enough oxygen to think straight? Whiskey, sir, always whiskey."

"Eat your bun and listen, Duff."

Quickly, Humph explained there were now three Broadway murders. He admitted everyone was at a loss as to who committed them.

"However, I'm not asking you to figure that out. What I want is for you to find out if there is mob money behind Broadway shows. There's one producer nobody seems to know, yet he's put money into at least two shows, if not three. His name is Jacob L. Burley."

"With a name like that, he's no respectable New York mobster. Maybe he owns a couple of rides on Coney. Something tells he's got a double chin."

"Get serious for a moment, for Christ's sake, Duff."

Humph explained that Burley seems to be an unknown, despite his money.

"No one had even heard of him two years ago. Is he just a Broadway-loving gangster or does he have another agenda? And why are his shows, at least his actors, being targeted?"

Duffy stuffed the rest of the sweet roll in his mouth, then washed it down with bourbon.

Humph suggested they head down to their old precinct and start asking around about Mr. Burley.

"Now?" said Duffy.

"You read my mind. We'll dredge up some whiskey on our return. All that counts this morning is that we plant the seed."

They set out on foot for the old precinct station, where both had served as cops, Duff rising to detective on the strength of his work helping solve the biggest case in Humph's career, the 1927 bootlegging, kidnapping and murder case. Humph was glad to see that the instant Duffy set foot in the precinct station he was greeted like a long-lost friend. Duff frantically waved his hands to pooh-pooh the acclaim. They made their way upstairs to the homicide division.

"Best start at the top," Duffy said. "We'll talk to the patrol boys at the pub later."

While Duffy wound his way through the rows of detective desks, shaking hands, slapping backs, Humph phoned Rebecca.

"Just wanted to say I haven't forgotten you. Remember the Irish cop?

"How could I forget him?"

"Well, I've asked him to try to track down the mystery mob money man, Burley. He hasn't heard of him but Duff's a bulldog. It's a start, I hope. I'll stay at home tomorrow if you want to meet."

Rebecca said she had no new information.

"I would be good to talk anyway," said Humph, hanging up as Duffy waved him over to a detective's desk.

Duff introduced him to a scrawny, mousy-looking man named Henry Higgins.

"Hank is the precinct's best mob guy," Duffy said, then turning to face the detective, he added, "This is not a knock on you, Hank, but you look so non-threatening you get to go places I can't go and people figure it's safe to yak at you."

"No offense taken," the little man said, but he wasn't smiling.

"Tell my friend Humph what you know about Brumley. By the way, does he have a double chin?" Duffy couldn't help himself. Humph knew that and he hoped Henry did.

Humph offered his hand to Henry, who leaned forward and shook it. Humph immediately thought that the guy wouldn't be much help in a fist fight. No grip at all.

When Henry spoke, his voice was surprisingly penetrating. There wasn't a hint of hesitancy or shyness.

"Brumley is the real deal. A made man. His forte was ingratiating himself with financiers. He would admit openly that he was looking for inside deals and would pay handsomely for the tips."

He paused to see Humph's reaction. He made it clear that Duffy wasn't his kind of cop.

"Since the crash, brokers have to be a lot more careful but Wall Street is Wall Street. Money people just changed suits and pursued the same illegal schemes. Brumley seemed sophisticated and is accepted in the bars the Wall Street boys frequent."

"Any known Broadway connection?" Humph asked.

"At the moment, all I know is that with the Depression money has dried up. Investment in Broadway is way down. Maybe Brumley is riding in as a knight in shining armor."

The humble Henry Higgins was nobody's fool, thought Humph.

"If ticket sales are so far down, what does he have to gain?"

Henry remained silent. Finally, Duff broke the silence,

"That Brumley bugger is seeking control of Broadway. If he has a couple of hit shows in this mucky market, people will be looking for his money to set them up for their shows. If the market ever comes back, he'd be sitting pretty, double chin and all."

"Duff," said Humph, with all sincerity, "you never cease to amaze me." Even Henry had to smirk.

As Duffy and Humph walked out and back to Bowery, Duff read Humph's mind and said:

"The way I figure things, if those actor murders were aimed at scaring away Brumley, the people doing that have to be mighty sure of themselves. Why would they give a crap right now about mob money. The only important thing is that Broadway goes on. Who could organize these assassinations? Who would dare take on the mob? Whoever they are, if you consider how they killed these actors, they're a skilled and nasty lot."

Humph suddenly wished he'd never asked Eve to keep her ears open about mob involvement.

"To the pub, sir."

Humph didn't feel the enthusiasm a visit to their old stomping grounds used to engender. First of all, the booze wouldn't be free in a few months. When Prohibition ended, cops wouldn't be able to seize a bar's stock and deposit it in what the precinct laughingly called the "evidence locker". What once looked like a lifetime supply of hooch for precinct members would soon be all but exhausted. In fact, to ensure their supply of booze lasted a while longer, the bar was already charging a token fee for drinks. Humph couldn't help but think that if the city paid flatfoots a living wage they wouldn't be so thirsty.

Nevertheless, when the barkeep shooed away a cop on the corner barstool to make way for Humph, his chest heaved with a brotherhood kind of pride. His life as a PI was a thousand times more gratifying but the blue brotherhood had overtaken a patch In his heart. On more than one occasion, he wondered whether a woman in his life could reclaim that patch, the pre-copper patch. He even wondered whether he wanted to expunge that loyalty,

Duffy took charge of the floor. He offered a free belt—whiskey or beer—to anyone who knew the name Brumley. There were no takers other than a cop who knew a Brumley who ran a funeral home in Hackensack, New Jersey.

His next contest was a free belt for anyone who'd ever gotten rough with a Broadway producer.   Several cops raised their hands.

The first cop said a big shot of some kind arrived in front of a Broadway marquee one night and started to exit his limo.

"Two lugs moved in and shoved him back in. One of them, the bigger of the two, got in the limo next to the big shot. Ten minutes later, the big guy got out and the limo drove off. Mr. Money Bags never got to see a play that night."

Another cop said he saw something similar this winter. Some muscle blocked the stage entrance to a show called *American Dream*. They let the actors in but not the guys in suits."

Duff turned to Humph.

"Smells like mob to me."

"Where do we go from here," Humph asked.

"I think we should have a chat with that famous Broadway aficionado, the double-chinned Mr. Brumley."

CHAPTER 13

REBECCA didn't phone beforehand. She knocked on Humph's door at 8:25 a.m. Humph was already up, which is why he noted the time of the knock. The knock was firm but not overly aggressive so it wasn't Duffy. Humph was relieved because Duffy in the early morning was like a 4.3 earthquake.

As usual, her brown eyes held his gaze as she entered. However there was no evident smile or greeting. He had become used to that. It made little sense to him that a talented make-up artist, and a beautiful woman, would present that kind of front. Was it armor or just distrust of white men who asked too many questions?

"I've found someone who might be of use. She's a dancer. Like your Eve, she's performed in vaudeville, in strip joints and in plays off Broadway. She says a very well-dressed guy approached her a few months ago. He wanted extracurricular services but first needed some information. He made it clear that he would take her services whether she agreed or not, but he would only offer money if she gave him the information he wanted."

"What did the bastard want to know?" asked Humph.

"He wanted to know whether she had ever met a producer named Bainsworth. He wanted to know where he lived. He wanted to know what shows he'd invested in."

"Why would he ask a dancer that?" asked Humph.

"I guess he knew that money people tend to stick their heads in during casting and rehearsals to see where they're money's going. Anyway, as you put it, this 'bastard' said he wanted to meet the Bainsworth guy face to face. He made it clear in so many words that if she couldn't arrange that she would never perform on Broadway again."

"You're destroying my fantasies about life on Broadway," said Humph.

"When I met her," Rebecca said, "the mere mention of this guy's name sent her into convulsions. 'Why me?,' she wanted to know."

"Six months before, she said, she lived on a farm in Idaho. She picked potatoes day and night. What could she possibly know about people like Bainsworth or, for that matter, this guy who came out of nowhere and stared her down backstage? She said she only got the job because she had a great smile and an even greater behind. She said the production was garbage and her 'farm girl assets' were the only reason she got the job."

Humph sat silent for a while.

"Could it be that this well-dressed bastard with all the questions about that producer guy, Bainsworth, might be working for Brumley?"

Rebecca said she had no idea.

"What possible connection could there be?" she asked.

"Just guessing but to my way of thinking, a known mob

guy would try to stay behind the scenes when it came to buying a big hunk of a Broadway show. It wouldn't look good in the papers. It might even hurt ticket sales..."

Rebecca finished his thought.

"So he'd send a lackey to set things up and twist some arms. Maybe he'd try to convince the show's owner or owners that they needed a bigger, more expensive star, or, to make sure the show doesn't open until it's perfect, they had to run it past theatergoers in even more cities than planned originally."

"Exactly, Rebecca. He'd try to convince them it was crucial to even hire the best make-up artist in showbiz."

For the first time since Rebecca knocked on Humph's door, she smiled.

Humph announced that he needed to revisit Det. Henry Higgins, the gangland expert Duff introduced him to at the precinct.

He told Rebecca she was welcome to accompany him but she said she had to get to work. Before leaving, Humph phoned the precinct to make sure Higgins was there. On the way, he put his massive arm around the diminutive Duffy and led him down the stairs to Bowery. By the time they got to the precinct, Duffy had finished complaining about the early hour.

After entering the station, it took almost 10 minutes to get up one flight of stairs to the detective's desk because once again Duffy was besieged by the cops he'd worked with for so many years.

"Can't stay away, can you Duffy" and "See ya at the precinct pub, I hope."

Duffy pretended to be annoyed—"I'm a busy man or have you all gone blinkin' blind?" By the time he got to the top of the stairs, Humph noticed that he was smiling.

Humph sat down in front of Higgins while Duffy swiped a chair from the next desk and positioned it next to Humph, who was exchanging greetings with the little man.

"So what have we got," Duffy demanded without bothering to say hello.

"What we've got, Duffy," said Humph, "is questions. Too many questions." He then turned from Duffy and faced Higgins.

"I'm inclined to agree," said Higgins. "We've got three murders of actors in just weeks when we've never had a single one before. We know that two of them were committed my middle-aged society women and the third apparently committed by some kind of militant Haitian woman. The chances of two bluebloods going looney and getting lethal within days is a coincidence difficult to accept."

"On the surface, there's no connection, but there has to be," said Higgins.

"The only connection I see," said Humph, "and I admit this is a reach, is that the dead actors performed in productions wholly or partly owned, possibly, maybe, perhaps, by a mobster. We think his name is Brumley. I was hoping you'd have some background on him, detective."

"Your instincts are good, Humphrey." Humph ignored the compliment and all but ordered the detective to call him "Humph, simply Humph."

"Of course, I believe you've told me that before," Higgins said.

"Well, as to your theory, I don't have a definitive answer, but I can say that, for a mobster, Brumley is an odd duck. We've known of him for some years but he seems almost on the periphery of the city's hard-core gangster world. We've never been able to connect him to any violent affairs. We nailed him once for insider trading, you know, that nasty practice engaged in by wealthy investors and brokers alike until the crash of '29.

"I'm sure he still dabbles. As to what he contributes to maintain his place as a made man is less than clear. Rumor has it that he enjoys real estate fraud among other endeavors. I heard but couldn't prove that he has sold more than a few acres of swamp land, here in Manhattan as well as Long Island and Brooklyn. He would sell some to buyers too rich and busy to inspect their new property before signing on the dotted line. Had they done so they would have learned their land was useless unless drained and filled in. For other properties, he admitted up front that they were swampland but he egregiously downplayed the cost of recuperating the land and instead emphasized the great potential profits of building on it. He would sell this kind of land as the perfect way to turn yourself into a real estate tycoon."

Duffy offered that the name Brumley was ideal for that kind of fraud.

"A man with such an unfortunate name was surely harmless," Duffy said. "His ancestors in all likelihood spoke all plummy like and pretentious. Maybe our man Brumley can turn it on as needed to impress us Colonials."

Duffy, thought Humph, was just being his Irish self, but since Brumley was not associated with violence, perhaps he had more refined means of convincing people.

Humph suddenly asked Higgins:

"If someone was trying to cripple Broadway shows that Brumley was involved in, why go to the trouble and risk of having actors murdered? Why not just take out Brumley?"

"Good point," said Higgins.

Duffy stepped up to summarize their point:

"So we're right back where we started. Three loopy broads and a partridge in a pear tree."

"Not quite," said Humph. "This can't be a coincidence. Two if not all three killings are linked."

Higgins agreed.

"Maybe Brumley has nothing to do with the murders. If so, there's got to be another explanation, another connection. In the meantime, Humph, I'll do a little digging into what makes Brumley tick."

Once outside, Duff turned left toward to "Precinct Pub".

"Whoa!" Humph said.

"I have to go back. I forgot to ask Higgins a couple of things."

Duffy chose to wait outside.

Humph went upstairs and caught Det. Higgins just as he was putting on his jacket and heading toward the door.

"Sorry detective but I forgot to ask two questions. One, is the woman in Murder No. 1, Clarissa, is she still in Bellevue? Has anyone tried to interview her again. Is she sane enough to help us out? Does she actually remember killing the young man?"

"No," said Higgins. "We haven't checked up on her. I can guess your second question. What's the latest on the so-called Vanderbilt lady. A pretender? The real McCoy? The real culprit? Did she truly act alone?"

"Precisely, detective."

"You're absolutely right to want such answers. All I know is that she's at liberty with a stipulation that she remain in New York."

Humph nodded.

"Why haven't you asked a third question? The Haiti connection."

Humph admitted he had assumed the police had no leads.

"Don't know why I thought that but despite evidence that a Haitian man and a Haitian women followed the young man at some point, there's no evidence to my knowledge linking the knifing to them. However, detective, tomorrow or the next day, I plan to go to Harlem and start knocking on doors. The Broadway show the young man was in...the show's make-up artist knew him slightly and has offered to help me in Harlem. She's Puerto Rican and might have easier access."

Higgins smiled and extended his hand to Humph.

"I think we would have made a good team."

As soon as Humph stepped back on the sidewalk, Duffy said, "Enough is enough. All roads at this hour lead to…"

"I know, I know. My compass always pointed in that direction when I was a beat cop at end of shift."

Duffy faced forward and set a military man's pace.

Humph didn't want to wake up hungover the next day. Rebecca had been good enough to help him out but, in the end, he was the detective who would know how to ask the right questions, supposedly.

He knew he knew little about Rebecca. He had encountered people like her before, usually women. They didn't need anyone's approval. It was if they had an inner navigator who always knew where due north and the truth lay. It wasn't personal when she made no comment about one of his suggestions, or when she contradicted him. She would know somehow that she was right and raising her voice to insist or protest his disagreement wouldn't add to that truth.

He was still thinking of Rebecca when they got to the tavern.

"Make way!" Duffy said in a stentorian voice.

He was greeted with mock salutes and a chorus of *Danny Boy* by his former colleagues.

Duffy thrust his hands in the air and cried, "Shut your yaps!" When the last voice petered out, Duffy announced, "You'll not squeeze a tear out of my eye because that bloody song was penned by a damned Englishman, some lawyer or something. No more Irish than that Statue of Liberty lass who hangs about in the harbor."

Several pairs of hands clapped.

"Bravo, Duffy. One of your better entrances," said a sergeant.

Humph said he'd second the motion.

"Sassenachs, the lot of you," declared Duffy, all but spitting out the word.

"Whiskey," he told the barkeep.

Humph waved off the glass the bartender was about to plunk in front of him.

"Not today, my friend."

"What's eating you all of a sudden?" Duffy asked Humph.

"I'll tell you what. We've got three murders, three dead actors, and absolutely no idea who killed them or why. We're all just speculating, sitting around and speculating. It's time to start investigating for real. I'm going to Bellevue, Duffy. I want to see if that crazy society woman is still crazy. I don't buy her story about killing the young actor."

"Christ, Humph, let a man finish his glass for heaven's sake."

Humph flagged a cab. As they made their way north to 26ᵗʰ Street and First Avenue, Duffy did his best to avoid paying half the fare.

"Humph, you're forgetting that I'm a retired gentleman, while you are on business. I'm just keeping you company. Why should I pay anything?"

"Because," answered Humph, "you're bored silly at home. You want to be on the case. And you want to maintain access to my booze table. You're cheaper than a Scotsman."

By the time they stepped onto the sidewalk in front of the huge hospital complex, Duffy had capitulated. He handed Humph $1.50.

Humph asked for directions to the Pavilion for the Insane. A young man in a white coat pivoted to his left and pointed to the building. He never uttered a word. Inside the entrance, Duffy pulled out his souvenir police badge, given to him at retirement.

"This might make it easier to get to see the looney lady," he told Humph.

"It might be easier, Duff, if we don't refer to her as Looney Lady. Her name is Mrs. Clarissa Sidwell, a respectable citizen in most people's minds."

They started to walk down a corridor but had to halt when a nurse called out from behind them:

"Hey, boys, about face. You need to sign in, tell me who you want to see and wait for me to get a doctor to say OK."

Duff pulled out his badge again and flashed it before the nurse. She wasn't impressed.

"Still got to get a doc's OK."

Suddenly three doctors appeared at the nursing station. The nurse pulled the sleeve of one of them, a young, serious-looking man.

"These gentlemen are cops," she announced.

Humph stepped in between them and explained who they needed to see.

"Before we go to her," Humph said, "can you tell us anything about her state of mind now that she's been in your care for a while?"

The doctor had little to say. Duffy was just trying to memorize the twists and turns as they turned down one hallway after another, then mounted a flight of stairs. His years of work as a cop had taught him it was always a good idea to have a plan of escape even if you didn't think you had any real reason to suspect you'd need it.

Instead of entering Mrs. Sidwell's room, they entered a common area. An obese woman at the far wall, by the window, played Scott Joplin's *Maple Leaf Rag*. She did justice to it, Duff thought and said so to the doctor, causing him to stop to face the patient at the piano.

"Oh yes. That's the only thing she does well in life. She identifies with the composer, a Mr. Scott Joplin, because they share a birthplace, Texarkana, Arkansas. What I've never had the courage to tell her is that Mr. Joplin spent his last days in this very asylum in New York just as she is doing. His dementia was caused by syphilis. Hers? Science doesn't know. I tell myself she could be this happy on the outside only if she had a room with a window and, before it, a piano. Watch her, sir. Look at her face. Only a child could look that happy."

Humph was impressed by the doctor's knowledge of non-medical matters as well as his evident compassion for his patients. For some reason, Humph had been prepared to think of him as a warden or jailer of sorts.

Duffy was happy to listen to the Joplin rag, which had become an enormous hit not so many years before. Imitators of the style were everywhere now. Listening to the infectious music enabled him to imbibe aggressively without a tinge of sadness floating in to ruin the evening.

The doctor tapped him on the shoulder and led him and Humph to the other side of the room. There was Mrs. Sidwell. The doctor introduced them.

"Call me Clarissa," she said. Since eliminating her selfish, money-obsessed husband from her mind years ago, her call to arms had become her standard greeting to all and sundry, lovers and lap dogs wanting her money. Humph guessed that each usage of "Call Me Clarissa'" eliminated the Sidwell curse on her life. She clearly remembered meeting Humph. She was ensconced in an easy chair but her body stiffened as she stared up at Humph as if suddenly gazing into the eyes of a savior.

"How are we today, Clarissa, dear?" said the doctor, placing a hand softly on her left shoulder.

"Why do people keep saying I killed my beautiful young lover? Doctor? Tell me."

"Don't you remember, Clarissa, you said you did. You said you lay on top of him and slit his throat."

Clarissa's face changed. She was angry.

"Don't you know how beautiful he was? What woman could take the life of that Haitian angel? Tell me…You don't know? I'll tell you, doctor. The answer is 'No woman.'"

"Why did you say you did it?"

Clarissa sank back into her chair. Minutes passed. The doctor held his arm out to make sure neither Humph nor

Duffy fractured the silent thoughts of Mrs. Sidwell.

Finally, she spoke.

"Because when I saw his body on the floor, I wanted to die with him."

The doctor continued to hold out his hands to silence the two investigators.

"Until that beautiful man entered my life, I was dying every day. My so-called husband had ostracized me. I wasn't even a physical body to him, someone to plunder for his pleasure alone. He never called me by name anymore. He refused all my calls. He never took me anywhere. He got me a servant, my very own. It was like he was saying, now you have everything. You have position, you have wealth. Now suffocate so I can quietly move on with my life without you."

Humph suddenly wondered whether instead of stabbing him she had found him dead and lain on top of him in utter despair. His death meant that her life was now snuffed out, just as her husband wished. "Suffocate and disappear," he'd said.

She could still attend society events alone with a ready excuse that hubby dearest was working to brighten Broadway's white lights. But in time it meant that she was invited less and less.

There was more life at Bellevue with Scott Joplin's rags on the daily menu.

The doctor said to Humph, "I don't think she knows where she is, but not knowing doesn't seem to bother her now. Now and then she calls out for her butler but to explain his abscene ends up saying he must be running an errand for her."

Humph asked Clarissa who introduced her to the young actor. She seemed totally stymied by the query. Her brow furrowed to the extreme, she gazed at Humph. Humph knelt down in front of her, to make it easier for her to look into his eyes.

Her left hand reached out to his. Her hand was so small and her touch so light he didn't realize right away what she'd done.

Minutes later, she said:

"It was a gentleman named, I think, Willy or Walton. Yes, Walton. He said he knew the boy and said the young actor would give the world to meet a woman such as myself. He said I was someone at the very heart of New York society, the kind of woman who could serve as his patron and welcome him once and for all to America. He said I was a Haitian boy's dream. Then he showed me a photograph, a publicity shot for the show. I melted. He was heaven sent. So, so beautiful."

More than ever, Humph was convinced that Clarissa didn't murder the young actor. He doubted she could kill anybody. He also realized that he had seen firsthand how wealth had nothing whatsoever to do with happiness. Maybe, he thought afterwards, as he and Duffy walked back to First Avenue, he would no longer hate rich people so much. They were cruel and crazy-stupid like the rest of us.

CHAPTER 14

LATER that day, Humph got a call from Rebecca.

"I just met Eve on set. She is dying to know how we were doing with the investigation. I told her, 'Not well. All roads lead away from Rome.'"

"What does that mean, Rebecca?"

She laughed and said Eve asked the same thing.

"What I meant was that if our killers are in Rome, all investigative roads seem to be taking us away from finding out who committed these murders."

Humph humored her. "Got it. Got it."

He told her he and Duffy went to see the society woman in Bellevue. He said he was more convinced than ever she could no more kill a man than choose the wrong fork for dessert.

"However, she came up with a name, Walton, a man she said introduced her to the young Haitian actor. She didn't know anything about him, not even a first name. She said he was charming. He said the young man would love to meet a noble lady of her kind."

He added that Duffy was going to ask around with his police buddies to see if the name Walton rings any bells. In the meantime, he suggested, today would be a good day to ring a few doorbells in Harlem in search of a neighborhood with a lot of Haitians.

Rebecca agreed to join him.

They met mid-afternoon. She was wearing a billowy, multi-colored skirt and large earrings.

"Haitians are like us Boricuas. They love color. They think Americans either have no taste or are color blind."

Humph stopped walking. "Bo-ri-whats?"

Rebecca laughed.

"You can call us Puertorriqueños or Boricuas. Chose the term your tongue prefers."

"Maybe later, Rebecca. We're going in search of Haitians. I can pronounce that with ease."

At one point, as they stood in line to board a streetcar on Third Avenue that would take them to their hunting ground, Humph found himself a few feet behind Rebecca. There was a slight breeze that caused her voluminous skirt to wave to one side, like a proud flag of sorts. She was rather beautiful, he thought.

As they approached their destination, just past her street, Rebecca pointed out local landmarks. In the distance, they could make out a market and despite the distance from the streetcar the music from the market made everyone on the streetcar feel a little bit more alive. Humph could tell Rebecca felt at home.

Once they got off the streetcar, Rebecca suggested they walk up and down a few streets, starting at Fifth Avenue and working their way east to the river.

Had Duffy been his partner this afternoon instead of Rebecca, they would have first sought out a saloon.

"Let's look around for an hour then grab some street food," Rebecca suggested, eyeing him from a distance of no more than a foot.

Humph nodded. "Had she read my mind?" Humph wondered.

It was actually closer to two hours before they stopped to rest. Because they were knocking on tenement doors one after the other, they had attracted a following. It grew with each stop. Even a switch to a street further east deterred no one. An alarm bell had sounded, it seemed.

Occasionally, Rebecca glanced back. Unlike Humph, she wasn't alarmed by the mini mob. Finally, to Humph's relief, she walked into the middle of 108th Street, a stone's throw west of Third Avenue, and pirouetted, making her skirt fly in a perfect circle. The gesture was greeted with more than a few cheers. She then held her right hand high and yelled,

"Viva Puerto Rico!"

The crowd returned the words and began to disperse.

"Now," Rebecca said, "we must face the fact that we've gotten nowhere. We've met some Haitians but when we mention Broadway, most of them look puzzled. When we mention murder, they ask us to leave. They obviously just want to live quietly and attract no attention from the white man's world in the place they've chosen for refuge."

Humph hated the fact that they'd never gotten far enough in a conversation to ask if any of them knew about Haitian militants in New York, ones who wanted the U.S. out of their homeland, ones who were ready to murder anyone pretending to approve of the American presence there.

"Time for food," said Humph.

Rebecca pointed west. They made their way back to Lexington Ave. A few blocks south they found two food vendors, one on each side of the street. On the west side, near the food stand, a mustachioed man with slick-backed black hair, was singing ballads. Before him, on the sidewalk a few feet away, was a flat-top hat. There were coins, but very few, inside.

Rebecca walked right up to him the instant he finished singing.

"*Buenas, señor.*"

"*Hola preciosa.*"

Rebecca dropped two quarters into his hat. Humph would not have been embarrassed if she'd dropped a dime.

She asked if he knew any Haitians in the neighborhood.

At first he shook his head and said, "Not really, *cariña.*"

Humph's jaw dropped as Rebecca pressed even closer to the singer.

"I really, really need help," she said. All the while her brown eyes fixed on his. From a distance of a foot or so, it seemed to Humph that her pupils were growing larger. Brown magnets? Whatever the effect was, the singer capitulated. Humph put a dollar in his hat to make the spell last.

The singer indicated they should follow him. They made their way to Broadway and walked north for at least a mile, Humph calculated, starting to puff. They stopped at a dance hall just south of 145th Street. They stepped inside. The singer took a corner seat by the window and beckoned them to join him. There were only two other customers, sitting next to the counter at the back.

When they were seated and coffee had been served, he said he knew what her questions had meant, though he had claimed ignorance.

"I often perform here. The clientele is almost 100 percent Latino. Not just Puerto Ricans but Mexicans, Cubans, Colombians. Name it. We are all one here when the music starts. I can't describe the feeling. Like them, I am a very long way from home. You're from Puerto Rico, yet you speak to me in English. I know you understand."

Rebecca didn't shrink from his stare. She nodded her understanding.

"It's time," Rebecca said after a moment. "We need your help."

Just then, the band launched into a merengue. Incredibly loud, thought Humph. However, even he felt like moving his tree-trunk legs. But this was not the moment to ask Rebecca to dance.

The street singer leaned close to Rebecca's ear and tried to make himself heard over the music. Its volume must have made him feel safe. No one could have overheard him. But from the other side of the table, Humph heard most of the words. He vowed to learn Spanish after the case. Anyway, he knew he'd learn everything later from Rebecca.

He had to wait until the band's set ended. The singer raised the back of Rebecca's hand to his face and got up. A second later, he had disappeared into the crowd on the dance floor.

Rebecca took a deep swallow of her boulevardier cocktail. Why, wondered Humph, would a Latin dance parlor serve such an absurd cocktail, made of equal parts of bourbon, compare and vermouth? Was he like Duff in the end, a dyed-in-the-wool male traditionalist, a creature from the last century? No matter, Humph finally decided, he was hungry.

Rebecca looked pleased with herself. She happily accepted Humph's hand and let him lead her to the door. Once outside, Humph was about to head north to the 145ᵗʰ Street subway station. She resisted gently and turned him south to a restaurant that seemed to hide its presence. The walk downhill to 137ᵗʰ Street was easy. She held his arm and led him through the door. They were in a Mexican restaurant. To his right as he looked into the small dining room was a dream-like mural. Floating Mexican faces and spirits. To his left, chairs and small tables. Before he felt oriented, an elegant Latino woman with drawn-back black hair, a hypnotically sexy white blouse and a bold red skirt, melted him with an ear-to-ear smile. She pointed to a table. He sat, like an automaton. Rebecca sat on the bench seat, positioning herself within inches of him.

"Would you like me to order?" she asked.

He nodded.

Rebecca figured Humph was in no mood for experimenting. She ordered tacos.

Before they arrived, Humph stared at her, hard.

"Well?" he said.

"Oh, I forgot you could not understand what the *cantante* was saying at the club. It was a gold mine, Humph."

"And you wait until now to tell me?"

"I didn't want to ruin your appetite."

Humph bit his tongue. His Eve understood his impatience but it would insult Rebecca. A voice told him not to do that. He paid heed.

When his beef taco arrived, he opened wide and took a Moby Dick-sized bite.

While the detective masticated, Rebecca said that the singer had told her that a white man named Walton Gagliardi had recently visited the club early one day when it was closed to the public. The infectious music still played but it was from a radio sitting on the bar. Gagliardi wanted to know who owned the club. He said he could create a star-filled future for the club if they could reveal the name of the person who ordered the killing of the young Haitian actor. The man was spooky, the street singer had said. And a bit scary. No one at the bar knew anything about it, or at least that's what they said.

"Why would this guy think a Latin dance bar in Harlem would know anything about the killing of a Haitian actor?" Humph asked, plunking down his mostly eaten taco.

"You really were hungry," Rebecca said, pointing at the remains of the taco.

Apparently, said Rebecca, the Gagliardi guy had been involved in show business somehow. He said he had lots of connections with the right people, the money people downtown. As for the dead Haitian, he said he was just curious. He said he was idly wondering whether Harlem was where the Haitians lived. Our street-singer friend said the man's apparent ignorance just didn't add up and no one bought it. He must have had another motive for his questions.

Humph leaned back in his chair, dangerously. Suddenly, he understood why Rebecca thought the interview was worth bold. The name Walton, the very name the crazy society woman mentioned as the one who first introduced her to the young Haitian actor. Walton Gagliardi.

At the Mexican restaurant, they were almost right across the street from the downtown train. On the way home, Humph said he'd ask the boys in blue about this Gagliardi fellow. Humph found himself enjoying the 25-minute ride with Rebecca. They didn't talk much. Instead, Humph followed his practice of giving every fellow passenger the once over, looking for oddities in their appearance or manner, noting the ones who had despair or anger hiding behind their eyes. Rebecca seemed comfortable doing much the same. When they got off at 14th Street, Humph offered to accompany her home to Avenue B. He disguised the offer by saying he was curious about the state of Tompkins Square Park since the tent-city police raid.

When they got to Avenue B, Humph walked her to the door and then headed home without a peek inside the park.

CHAPTER 15

HUMPH slept poorly again. They had made some progress but in the end little was making sense. He had already ruled out the coocoo high society lady. The only thing about her that was possibly of interest was the fact that her husband was a Broadway money man.

As unusual as the other two murders of Broadway actors were, nothing tied them together apart from how the victims made their living, and from what his cop friends told him, there was nothing in their history to warrant death-by-hitman.

And even the latest man of interest, the mysterious Gagliardi, maybe he was just a businessman with enough money to get into showbusiness from the Harlem side of the ledger. No one had apparently heard of Gagliardi but the Harlem location rang a bell with Humph. The Cotton

Club, on 147th Street and Lennox Avenue, was known as the Aristocrat of Harlem. It was owned by a white man, a gangster, the infamous Owney "The Killer" Madden.

Humph had gone there with a woman who had been the only one he had fancied since the death of Eve's mother years before. Her name was Karena, one of the first female New York cops. They went there searching for clues about Eve's kidnapping.

The music was the best he'd ever heard but the whole place was "whites only". Black musicians did the entertaining. The place evoked a jungle atmosphere and the staff, black, was dressed as savages. Deep down, Karena, his date, was a tough cop but she wasn't born in the U.S. She soon told Humph to get her out of there.

Humph got out of bed and sat at his all-purpose table, which served as a desk and a dining room table, and a place to slouch when the day was taking a toll.

He was still half-asleep and nodding. Suddenly, the name Walton Gagliardi flashed before his eyes like a flashing Times Square advertisement.

Is it possible, he wondered, that this smooth-talking entrepreneur was involved more deeply than simply having introduced the society lady to the Haitian actor?

After downing his morning coffee with uncommon haste, Humph set out for the precinct station. He climbed the stairs two at a time, yelling back "Mornin', fellas" to the uniform cops on the first floor.

Damn, he thought, Det. Henry Higgins was not at his desk. Humph went behind Higgins' desk and sat. The other detectives were used to his presence. No one objected. Because Higgins was diminutive of stature, he had spun his desk chair to its maximum height. Humph felt like lord of the manor until he lowered it.

Twenty minutes later, Higgins arrived. Humph rose. Higgins sat. Several cops chuckled. Higgins all but disappeared behind his desk. Humph apologized and

Higgins stood again, patiently returning the chair to its previous height. Fortunately, thought Humph, Higgins was not inclined to outbursts of annoyance.

"What have you got for me?" Higgins asked.

"Questions."

"About?"

"A certain Mr. Gagliardi, Walton Gagliardi."

The look on the detective's face suggested the name didn't ring a bell. Here merely commented that Walton and Gagliardi hardly seemed compatible as names.

Humph explained that on a trip to Harlem he had discovered that Gagliardi was trying to buy outright or at least by into a popular Latino dance club with the promise of investing major money and showbiz experience into the venture. When he asked the owners whether they were interested, he got a blunt *Non, para nada* in reply. No dice and no explanation. They turned their backs and turned up the music.

"They either have a very good thing going and don't need outside money, or they simply don't want to lose control of it to a white man who clearly didn't understand a word of Spanish."

"Why," asked Higgins, "was that of any interest to you?"

Humph was stumped.

"That's the thought I woke up with this morning."

Higgins, usually polite, stared at Humph for uncomfortable seconds.

"A detective, a man of facts, comes here to tell me about a question that was no more than accidental sleep excrement…"

Humph interrupted.

"Sorry, sorry, sorry," said the big man. Higgins thought he had witnessed something strange, a giant expressing boy-like regret.

"Let me back up, Henry. I'm trying to make sense of

three Broadway actors being murdered. At first, I thought I had legitimate suspects but investigations proved otherwise. I have nothing. I simply can't believe three different killers happened to single out Broadway actors. There's a mastermind somewhere, someone with a huge plan that can't possibly be defined by three individual murders of individuals who on their own account for nothing that involves money, profit, love, jealousy, revenge, gambling, you name it, Henry."

Henry didn't reply. He fiddled with a pipe and scanned three telegrams he'd found in his inbox. Humph knew he wasn't being rude. He was thinking. We all have our methods of distancing ourselves from situations far enough to allow logic to rule. If you look someone in the eye when responding, you are highly likely to debate and be confrontational. You are highly likely to utter preconceived opinions. It was a joy, thought Humph, to work with someone like Higgins. What a pair. He was like Jack in the Bean Stalk, Higgins was like one of the beans, but they were a team. Nature is strange.

Humph admitted he had not the slightest thread of evidence to suggest the man with an incompatible first and last name was a bad guy. However, he now revealed that Walton was the one who introduced the Haitian actor to the woman we at first thought killed him. The link between Gagliardi and the attempt to buy out the Latino club suggested there was more to him than met the eye. "I was hoping you could do some digging to find out who he really is," said Humph. "Is he a financial player or a criminal presence of some sort in New York. In short, did this businessman-investor have questionable tentacles?"

Shortly after Humph returned home, Eve appeared at his door.

"News, news, news!"

"And hello to you, too," said Humph with a grin. How he wished he was young enough again to feel things the way Eve did. He assumed she was joyous because she'd found the greatest novel ever written or the spiffiest blouse and skirt combo ever created.

"Sit," Eve ordered.

She plunked herself on is lap. It was a daughter's gesture. Her hand on is right cheek, she said:

"Rumor has it that the producer of my show. . . a sweet business guy from Staten Island." Eve looked at Humph and began to ramble. "Anyway, he once danced on Broadway until he hurt his back. That was many years ago. He never danced again. In fact, he can barely walk even now. Being backstage with us seems to ease the pain."

"That's tragic, Eve, but what did he tell you?"

"He said he may have to leave us. I swear there were tears in his eyes. I know you're going to say he doesn't sound much like businessman but Broadway does that to people. We all have stupid dreams. That's why we go to the shows. That's why some businessmen invest. It's not always about profit alone."

Humph was glad Eve found passion in life but he wasn't much touched by her revelations.

"You're not understanding, are you, Dad."

They stared at each other a moment, then Eve, impatient, blurted out that her producer was somehow being forced to relinquish control of the show. "How or why, I don't know."

After a light lunch at his place, they went for a walk. Despite the rumble of everyday New York, the Lower East Side still offered enclaves of calm. You had to know where to look. Humph and Eve found one, a tiny park that didn't deserve the name "park". Neither spoke for a while. Finally Humph asked if she thought it was possible that bad money was infiltrating Broadway.

"How would I know?" she replied again.

"Don't know. Just asking. I'm just wondering. You know, those three murders. They have to be linked somehow."

"Why would anyone want to corrupt Broadway?"

Humph took her by the shoulders and said:

"Money."

"But how would killing them mean money for the killer?"

Humph admitted that he had no clue at the moment.

"I don't know a damn thing about how those shows are financed, what kind of people invest, how easy or hard it is to make a profit. Need to do some research, obviously. But where to start?"

Humph admitted that while he had gone to see Eve's mother in vaudeville performances, he'd never gone to a Broadway show. Eve knew he worried that seeing even the happiest musicals risked making him sad.

"Let me try to find some people working on my show who would be willing to talk to you," Eve said. "I don't know how much help they will be in this kind of situation. They were undoubtedly as shocked by the murders as I was. Too close to home."

"Tell them I could use a beginner's course on Broadway," Humph said.

Back home, there was little he could do but wait for a call back from Eve about the Broadway tutoring or from Higgins about Gagliardi.

Frustrated by pacing in such a small apartment, Humph called Gerry Franklin at the *New York World*.

"Can you hook me up with your Broadway critic or your drama critic, whatever you call it?"

Always eager for a story to offer the City Desk, Franklin asked what scent his friend was tracking.

"Everything and nothing," Humph replied.

There was a long pause. Finally Humph said he was still trying to make sense of the murders of three Broadway actors.

"Thank you," Franklin said, with a theatrical tone of relief.

He then explained that the critic of course worked evenings, attending shows for the most part. If he was working in the afternoon, he was out interviewing actors, producers, writers, lyricists.

"You name it, Humph. Personally, I think he's a critic who thinks he could write better shows than the ones he reviews. A smidgin of ego, I'd say."

"My kinda guy," said Humph. "It makes my day to prick balloons."

"I'd so love to witness that," Franklin said. "I'll have him call you. I'll tell him it might lead to a juicy Broadway column, although only in the future. He might bite. I'll inform him that you're an ignoramus with regard to Broadway matters."

"Thank you, my friend. That would set him up nicely for a hard landing, as they say in today's new-fangled world of aviation."

CHAPTER 16

FOUR days later, an unseasonably cold day that somehow foretold of bad things happening, Humph found himself still at home. This case bothered him. In fact, they all did until they were solved, but now that Eve was a Broadway performer, the idea that innocent young, talented actors were being killed grabbed him to the point of pain.

Rebecca had called twice. The conversations were welcome but short, mostly because Humph was uncommunicative. Humph closely guarded his personal vault of emotions. Every time she hung up in frustration, he kicked himself. But in the end, he wasn't going to waste time becoming someone else. Too late in life, too impossible.

As usual, he went outside to buy the morning papers. Normally, he didn't look at them until he returned to his room and his precious morning coffee. Today was different.

"Dressmaker Drilled!" read the headline in one of the papers.

Once ensconced at his table, he read that a dressmaker employed by a Broadway costumer had been riddled with Tommy gun fire at the entrance to the store. Police could offer no plausible explanation as to why a young woman, who eked out an existence making costumes for theater productions, would have merited a mob rub-out.

Mistake in identity? Not likely. If the killers were after some other employee, or the owner, they would have targeted every square inch of the shop.

Three actors, one Broadway costumer. What next? Humph wondered.

The answer was not long in coming.

Rebecca showed up at his door. She was shaking. The trembling wasn't apparent at first but once she'd stepped inside the apartment, Humph detected it. He gently sat her down. It was the second time he'd seen her other than utterly composed. The first was the night the homeless people in Tompkins Square Park were being beaten by cops. In Harlem with him, she'd been a fearless interviewer, stepping in for Humph because she wasn't white and she knew that she could ask residents questions he couldn't.

Humph poured her a generous shot of rum. It was Dominican, not Puerto Rican, but he knew she needed something.

It took two lady-like swigs before Rebecca recaptured her composure.

"I overheard two guys talking at a show I'm working on, at the Amsterdam Theatre of all places."

"Why do you mean, 'of all places'?"

"Ever been to a Broadway show, Humph?"

"Vaudeville, yes, Broadway, no."

"Well the Amsterdam is on West 42nd. It's one of the oldest. Goes back to 1903. It's almost as old as you are."

The smart-aleck remark told Humph that Rebecca was back in form.

"Talk," he said.

"I was eavesdropping on two guys standing backstage. I've seen them before. They deliver some kind of theatrical supplies to shows. I not sure what. Maybe materials for sets, curtains, dancing shoes, paint, props, smoke-makers. I really don't know. Anyway…" Rebecca paused to hold out her glass for more rum.

"Anyway," she continued, "remember the guy who tried to buy out the Latin dance club in Harlem?"

"Yeah, the guy with the odd name. Walton Gagliardi, I think it was."

"Bingo," said Rebecca. She said the two shipping guys backstage were talking about that guy. One of them said something about the guy putting on the squeeze of some sort.

"To get closer to them, I tossed one of my make-up kits to the floor, just a few feet from them. I casually walked over and picked it up, taking my good old time examining the contents. The guys paid no heed to me. Beside the stage was hardly a quiet place. The director was arguing with the choreographer, telling him to shove his dancers closer together and further upstage.

"Out of view, you're saying?" bellowed the choreographer.

"Precisely," said the director. "When their moment comes and the orchestra strikes their cue, they will explode out of nowhere upstage left, dashing diagonally across the stage as if they're attacking our melancholy heroine downstage right."

Rebecca said she couldn't eavesdrop again until the director had finished hammering home his instructions to the choreographer.

"Finally, one of the supply guys said this Gagliardi guy told him just the other day that what he really planned to do was offer our guys so much money that we'd quit the union. He wants to break all the Broadway-related unions. I thought he was off his rocker until I learned that he has produced three shows on Broadway. Don't know why he quit that end of things."

Humph took in every word. Gagliardi was evidently a lot more than a businessman trying to step on happy toes in Harlem. He was much more ambitious and maybe a lot better at getting his way than the Latino licking he got at the club in Harlem would indicate.

He looked at Rebecca and raised his glass. She undoubtedly appreciated that Humph was praising her detective work. Humph admitted to himself later that he was raising his glass to a beautiful woman with a soft-spoken *determinación* he admired. It was a habit of Humph's. He would frequently hold his one-man review boards to examine his interactions with people during the day. The interrogation business was more one of listening and encouraging than telling, insisting and accusing. With his size, it was easy to be intimidating. Therefore effort was needed to reduce the threat.

"So what can we do about this guy?" Rebecca asked.

Humph rose and walked around the table until he got to Rebecca's chair, at which point, rather than forcing her to her feet, he reversed his way back to his chair across from her.

"You keep your Broadway nose in the air. I was going to say to keep it peeled but I guess that word is for eyes only."

Rebecca smiled. Humph was funny, even goofy, when he was relaxed. Very few people, she imagined, knew that.

"As for me, my dear, I'm going to shun my responsibilities and give our friend Duffy a painfully early wake-up call tomorrow morning. Should this Gagliardi guy have connections beyond the world of Broadway, Duffy has an unfailing nose."

"That must not necessarily be a blessing when living on Bowery," said Rebecca.

Humph laughed.

"His place is just as bad. Even the rats won't enter unless it's frigid cold outside."

Humph fiddled with his glass and snuck a peak at the woman across from him.

Clearly, she was in no hurry to leave. Humph also had do desire to say goodnight.

He lifted the rum bottle in invitation. Rebecca nodded with a tight little smile.

CHAPTER 17

THE next morning, it took Humph two sweet buns and 45 minutes to entice the grumpy king of Irish detectives to descend the stairs. Humph suddenly felt an urge to extricate him from the gloomy mausoleum of past cases, glories and ignominies. He had a long and genuine affection for Duffy but he also realized he wanted to take advantage of his instincts, contacts and unorthodox criminal imagination.

As had become a habit, they left Duffy's tenement and found the nearest bench in the morning sun.

"Talk," Duffy commanded. "I am not about to do so."

Humph took in the sun for a few moments. The thoughts that filled his mind at the outset had nothing to do with work. He was idly wondering whether he had the talent and patience to learn Spanish. Then, when Duffy suddenly belched, Humph turned his mind to the case.

He decided not to sound like he was reciting the events of a case incident. Instead, he opted for a manner better reflecting the world he was now living in with an actress-dancer daughter on Broadway and a make-up artist sought after by the stars of the Great White Way. He would, he decided, inject a touch of the theatrical in the hope of stirring the Irishman.

"What if I said...Duff? Are you listening?"

"I will when you come to your senses."

"By all that's holy in your bog back home, at least listen up."

"Screw you, laddie. Carry on."

"What if..." Humph began again. Despite seeing Duffy's eyes close, he decided to move along.

"What if I told you I suspect that someone, who has been spurned by the Great White Way in a manner yet to be determined, is determined either to take it over or destroy it? It's unimaginable, right, Duffy? Broadway is New York, even in this cursed Depression."

Duffy sat up. His slouch disappeared.

"I have one piece of advice, Humph. You seem to be treating Broadway as heaven-sent. It's not. It's about a bunch of eagle-eyed investors who corralled a bunch of well-meaning, albeit possibly talented, classical actors, you now, Shakespeare and all that shite, and sold them to the wolves, you know, the ignorant American public. Started way back In the last century. It's been a commercial con since the start."

"Why is that a con? They're just trying to make theater profitable?"

Duffy searched his pockets for a flask he didn't have.

"Because I work as hard as they do. They get rich. I don't. Only con men do that."

Humph could only think his friend was hungover. Or had age done that to him?

"Whatever, Duffy. I need your help. You don't have to

give a damn why anyone is doing what they're doing. I have a name. I think he's the man behind a lot of crap that's been messing up police blotters."

Duffy remained silent.

Finally, Humph said, "You're a cop or you're not, even in retirement. Which is it?"

"I never fucking retired. They booted me out. Screw them for eternity!"

"Exactly," said Humph, now standing over him. "So prove to those bastards that you're the best detective they ever had. I'm not asking you to work for those fools. Work for me and only me!"

Duffy, as tough as nails ordinarily, flinched.

Humph kept hovering. Duffy kept staring.

Finally, Duffy gave Humph a thumbs-up.

"Good man, Duff. I need you."

Duffy got up, squared his shoulders and asked Humph to point him in the right direction.

"To the headquarters of something called The Broadway League. They represent the major theater owners and companies who contribute to Broadway. They're the ones who negotiate with all the unions involved in shows, from set builders to stagehands and actors. Eve told me the League was formed just years ago. Since then pretty well everyone has joined."

"One big happy family?"

"I have no idea. Maybe they're just a bunch of businessmen cheerleaders. Maybe they just get together each season and pat themselves on the back and have a booze-up. Duff, I'd like you to find out and, in the end, find out about the Gagliardi guy I mentioned and any threats there may have been to Broadway ownership."

"Is that all?" asked Duffy.

"And, yeah. One more thing, Duff. Find out if Gagliardi is mob-connected and if anyone else labeled with the mob affiliation is hanging around backstage these days."

"You got me out of bed for this?"

"Always a pleasure," said Humph.

After about five minutes of walking toward their destination on Seventh Avenue just above 48ᵗʰ Street, Duffy suddenly stopped.

"What's the hour, Humph?"

Humph checked his time piece and announced that the hour was 9:42 a.m.

"Why?"

"I must inform you, you long-legged lunk, that it's a golden rule of mine to take taxis before 10 a.m. and after sundown."

Humph knew there was no point in arguing. He raised his hand higher than any other hand on the street and flagged a cab within minutes.

As they boarded the vehicle, Humph realized how much he depended on his pain-in-the-ass buddy. God help criminals, he thought. He was relieved to have gotten Duffy this far because he'd already made an appointment to see the president of the Broadway League, a Mr. Able King.

By the time the cab dropped them off in Midtown, Humph had finished filling Duffy in on the case, both facts, coincidences and pure speculation. Now, he hoped, they would have access to fresh leads. At worst, Humph hoped he could at least get confirmation that his fear that someone meant harm to Broadway was not that of a madman.

Abel King, the Broadway League's president, was, as Duffy described him later, decidedly a dapper sort of fellow. He wore a perfectly tailored brown, three-piece herringbone suit with a waistcoat that revealed an ornate but still elegant watch fob. For some reason, Humph was expecting someone who looked more theatrical. King raised his right arm, ushering the two detectives into his inner office.

Humph started right off by admitting that he'd been having nightmares about Broadway. With undisguised pride, he mentioned his daughter would soon be performing on a Broadway stage. A friend of hers, who also works on Broadway, admitted to having similar concerns.

"Concerns about what exactly, detective?" asked King.

"About the tragic and extremely alarming events of the recent past".

"I assume you're referring to the three murders of cast members."

"That's correct, sir. At first, I thought the three died at the hands of different people. But by the third incident, that possibility appeared absurd. We've investigated each of them thoroughly. However, what disturbs me now is a possible linking factor that I cannot support with a single fact. Yet this factor, the one providing a possible link among the three killings, is begging for an expert opinion, one that could either allow my hypothesis to stand on two legs or bury it once and for all."

Humph paused and the League president pointed to a pitcher of water on his desk with four glasses surrounding it. Duffy's hungover hand snuck in right behind Humph's.

Humph returned his water glass to the desk and remained standing. He wanted to pace, which was his practice when speculating and thinking out loud. It was also a practiced gesture that, where necessary, could intimidate. He had no need to daunt the president but he wanted to make sure the League boss didn't reject his ideas out of hand as being absurd conjecture.

"Here, sir, is what I call the first unlinked fact. We discovered that a man with an odd-sounding name, a Walton Gagliardi, had walked into a successful Latin dancehall way up in Harlem and tried to buy the place outright or at least buy a big hunk of it for a price the owners couldn't refuse. Long story short, they refused and sent him packing. We would have let the matter drop were it not for a conversation with a singer at the club who witnessed the man's attempt to buy the establishment. The gringo seemed to exaggerate his importance to an absurd degree, describing himself as a major theatrical figure in Midtown."

Humph retrieved his glass and went to the window behind the King's desk. Speaking to Seventh Avenue below, Humph said an acquaintance who works on Broadway, the one he'd mentioned before, told him she'd heard of this Gagliardi character. It turned out, he was…"

The executive interrupted.

"I know very well who he is. He was a producer until myself and the other board members booted him from the League. We found him guilty of attempting to circumvent several of our unions, first of all. It was less than three years ago when our producers and other money people first negotiated with the countless tradesmen and artists that make it possible to bring truly glorious shows to New York. We're inordinately proud of the goodwill extended by both sides in those early days. Though most of us are businessmen, we feel aligned with the workers' movement sweeping the nation in these hard times."

Duffy broke into soft applause.

"Bravo, sir. I don't know much about your Broadway doings but I never thought I'd hear a fancy man of affairs trumpet a cause of the common man. Bravo to you, sir."

Humph nodded to the League president and looked down at his friend approvingly.

Clearing his throat and turning back to the office window, Humph continued.

"Have you or your people uncovered any evidence or even heard of the possibility that Gagliardi is connected with mob money. My theory, unsupported by any facts whatsoever, is that Gagliardi not only was seeking to, as you might say, set the stage for a future of illegal profiting but is now seeking revenge on Broadway itself. My most absurd fantasy, sir, came to me in the middle of the night not long ago. I sat up in bed and told myself that Gagliardi, with the help of mob money, wants to dominate Broadway as a celebrity producer, reaping in hundreds of thousands of dollars for himself and his investors, or, failing that, destroying Broadway."

Humph knew those comments would be met with silence. He let the astonishment hang in the air before resuming:

"If Gagliardi somehow found enough scabs to lock out the unions and associations, and if he menaced other producers into following suit, could he not shut down the Great White Way as America knows it? If he is indeed mobbed up, would he not have the resources to do this?"

The League president looked up at Humph. Dumbfounded.

Humph circled his desk once, then sat next to Duffy, who had a glint in his eye.

It was the president's turn to get to his feet. He nodded at Humph, then walked past him to the door to his office.

While they awaited his return, Duffy said:

"There's hope for you yet, lad."

Humph was threatening Duffy with a sirloin steak-sized backhand when they heard the office door open.

"Gentlemen," said the president, "I have someone to introduce to you. You fellows probably speak the same language. This is Arnold Ottinger. He was a private investigator before he came to us and before that he made a hobby of observing the comings and goings on Atlantic Avenue. I've never been there but Atlantic City seems to hold an attraction for people with questionable funding and outsized appetites."

King turned to face Ottinger. To Humph and Duffy he said:

"I hope you don't mind but I took the precaution

of having Mr. Ottinger eavesdrop on us. So he knows the particulars of your nightmare."

Humph was relieved that the League president obviously didn't think him mad.

"Does the name Walton Gagliardi mean anything to you?" King asked Ottinger.

Ottinger said the name meant nothing but said that fact didn't mean much.

"The mob has more tentacles than a promiscuous pod of octopuses."

Duffy laughed out loud and the Broadway detective smiled in return.

"However," Ottinger continued, "I know the mob has entertained the idea in some form or another. Back in '29, I wrangled a job as a waiter at a shindig facilitated by none other than the political boss of political bosses in South Jersey, the endlessly corrupt and all-powerful Enoch "Nucky" Johnson. I suppose 'shindig' isn't quite the right word. Nucky's boys had laid the table and turned down the sheets for a national conference of organized crime, held at one of his luxury hotels. I think the whole town was so corrupt that the mayor was pissed off that he wasn't invited."

Ottinger said all the baddest of the bad boys were there: Masseria family lieutenant Charles "Lucky" Luciano and former Chicago South Side Gang boss Johny "the Fox" Torrio, with heads of the Bugs and Meyer mob, Meyer Lansky and Benjamin Siegel, and finally, the one and only Al Capone.

"Must have been the salt air that attracted them," added Ottinger with a bald cynicism that Humph and Duffy could relate to.

"Throughout Prohibition, Nucky made sure every ounce of hooch pointed toward the Jersey shore found a good home.

"You gotta remember that Atlantic City was boomtown

U.S.A. The whole world wanted to hear their heels clack and clunk on the boardwalk. It was in that spirit that these mob executives tossed around ideas of world domination… well maybe not quite world domination but domination of a whole slew of industries. Nooky's people wanted the city's entertainment business to rise to even new heights. The bigger it got the more booze sold, the more gambling, the more prostitution, all safe from the law thanks to Nucky and his muscle."

Not surprisingly, Ottinger added as a kicker, the plan included the idea of importing Broadway to Atlantic City in the summer when the theater scene in New York was idle. However, none of conference attendees knew how to pronounce or spell the word "union".

"Even though this was four years ago,' said Ottinger, "I clearly remember several voices blurting out at once that unions were as disposable as cigar butts and ugly broads. That was the second last day of the convention. The help was let go the next morning, me included, so that's all I know."

After a moment of silence, Duffy muttered:

"Well Humph, my lad, you're not mad after all. At least in their wildest dreams some nefarious lads were dreaming of conquering your beloved Broadway. For the record, I was betting that you were off your rocker."

His back to King and Ottinger, Humph gave Duffy the finger.

King said his assistant's information was interesting.

"However, at the moment it mostly means we'll simply have to ingratiate ourselves even more with the unions so we will always be in a position to top any offer a mobster might make them. In those four years since that conference in Atlantic City in '29, I've heard of no overtures whatsoever from questionably financed sources. I can only assume we're all on the up and up for now."

Humph stood again and looked squarely at King from

just across his desk. He was a good foot taller than the League president.

"Hold on. As potentially useful as Mr. Ottinger's espionage is, for the moment we still have no proof whatsoever that our iffy Mr. Gagliardi is connected to the mob in the first place or whether he has ever even tried to muscle in on a union that bargains with you. Not a shred."

Humph let the finality of his statement take hold.

"What I need from you, Mr. King, and any of your people who you think might be able to help, is 100 percent access to current contracts between your owner-partners and the associations and unions they deal with. I want to talk to anyone who has even given the time of day to Gagliardi, and I want to have a certain retired cop peruse the paperwork."

"Consider it done, sir. I'll draw up a letter of permission for you to tote around."

"And, please, a copy for Mr. Duffy."

King nodded. "If you plan to remain in Midtown for a few hours, you can pick up the letters this afternoon.

"Sounds good," said Duffy, reaching out to shake the president's hand. "The little lad here and I need a sit-down to confab while we wait."

As proper as the Broadway League executive appeared, he clearly enjoyed the sassy Irishman's humor. "Show business should have been his calling," he said to Humph as they shook hands.

Duffy led Humph to a diner on Eighth Avenue to kill time. On the way, Humph found a payphone. He borrowed the required five cents from Duffy and called Detective Higgins.

The detective said immediately that he had failed to uncover any information that would solve Humph's case or his own case. "Remember, the NYPD has three unsolved murders on its back because of you."

Before Humph could drop the phone, Higgins issued

his usually controlled laugh.

"Just giving you a hard time. Your investigation has turned this from three simple cases of unconnected murders, probably prompted by women and affairs of the heart, into a mob intrigue."

Humph didn't bite his head off. Instead, he complimented Higgins.

"I keep coming back to you because behind that disinterested exterior is a man who detests boredom and the obvious."

Higgins said there was no point oin having a quick conversation on the phone.

"Best get together here at the stationhouse."

"Duffy," interjected Humph, "might insist on the alternative precinct office."

"Do we need him?" asked Higgins.

"Absolutely," said Humph. "Though his nose might be a tad too red a tad too often, Duffy can nose around as well as any copper I've known. He knows all the right people, the disreputable people. They find it easy to think of him as one of their own. So much so that I've often wondered what Duff did before becoming a man in blue."

"Let's not ask," replied Higgins.

Humph returned to the diner.

Duffy was seated with a waitress. She was far past her prime but, of course, so was Duffy. Humph sat at their table but didn't interrupt. Duffy made no introductions. Within a couple of sentences it was apparent that the waitress was Irish through and through.

Finally Duffy rose.

"Give us a *póg*, girl."

She obliged, almost knocking him over with who full-body embrace.

"Sorry I took so long," said Humph sarcastically.

"In fact, dear Humph, I'd forgotten you'd left the table."

Humph explained the plan to meet Higgins the next

day.

"Shall we head back to the Broadway League?" Duffy asked.

"We'll probably be too early but I'd rather wait there than here, to be honest. Here I worry that you'll be kidnapped by a lass from a faraway land. Can't have that. I need you for the moment."

Duffy slapped him hard on the back. Humph scarcely felt it, but Duffy winced, shaking his hand.

The wait at King's office wasn't long. Humph scanned the agreements and the details about the unions, what products and labor they supplied to Broadway shows, the skills of the employees covered by the contracts, and, importantly, the dates when the current contracts expire.

"That," explained Humph, "was when our disguised mobster with the incongruous first and last names will make his pitch."

CHAPTER 18

THAT night, late, Eve appeared at Humph's door. She had just returned from Philadelphia where her show tested before a new audience.

"How did it go?"

"Not great, at least according to the reviews. However, the out-of-town critics seem to be pretty decent about allowing for the fact that we're on the road to perfect things for Broadway. They basically said they liked the execution by the cast but weren't too sure about the story itself. All that's out of my hands."

Humph didn't care about the critics.

"Do you realize that each tortuous step you take across that stage, from try-outs to rehearsals until you drop, to going on the road, you become more and more part of a world that the rest of American can only fantasize about? This road trip you just ended…it changed your identity forever. You've officially joined a fraternity, a sorority, a whatever. You can never lose your belonging. Even if your show flops, it doesn't mean you do."

Eve's eyes had grown wide as if her "dad" had made a speech at City Hall demanding Mayor O'Brien give her the keys to the city. Had he been drinking? He didn't smell as if he had.

"Damn!" she said. She then leaned over and gave him the awkward hug his size necessitated.

Eve had started referring to him always as Dad in the past couple of years. It wasn't a big step. In her heart, she'd been calling him that forever. She had also heard him "accidentally" referring to her as his daughter several times in the past.

"What's got into you?" she demanded.

"I've been spending a lot of time with your kind, theater people. You're rubbing off on me, you know, the fundamental dream business. America is so crippled now. I don't have words. No one does. Not even FDR. Dreams are worth more than dollars. Bucks buy a bowl of soup. They don't buy hope."

"Cops aren't supposed to think like that," Eve said.

He looked into her eyes. After a long moment, he kissed her cheek.

"A drink?"

"Sure, Dad."

For the next hour, Humph tried to clarify things in his own mind by attempting to explain what they now knew about the three Broadway murders, and what they suspected about mob involvement that might undermine Broadway somehow. Eve already knew, through Rebecca, about Gagliardi's ham-fisted attempt to take over the dance joint in Harlem. She never made a connection with mob involvement until Humph stated it was possible.

"What we need now," said Humph, "is evidence of attempts to subvert Broadway's unions, you know, yours, Actors' Equity, all the way through directors, designers, set-builders, costumers, name it. They're all game, I think, because any one of them can derail a production by refusing to agree to work for the offered wage."

Eve sat stone still.

She loved Humph's investigations: the frauds he uncovered, the high-society phonies he unmasked, the gangsters he derailed. But since she made the cut on a Broadway production, she had stopped believing for the first time in her life that she'd wake up the next day and find her world upside down. She knew that neither acting nor dancing would ever be a secure career but Eve now thought the worst was behind her. No more strip clubs, no more forced prostitution, no more two-night fill-in roles for a hungover Vaudeville performer and the stress of having practically no time to learn steps or lines. No more drunk asshole men with nothing in their brains but plenty in their wallets.

Broadway was the real thing in entertainment. The pinnacle. She didn't want to hear anything to the contrary.

But Humph continued. After a moment, he realized her eyes were turned inward. She wasn't hearing a thing he was saying.

He shut up and waited.

He understood what she was going through. Since the kidnapping and sex-trafficking six years ago, his beautiful Eve was close to being the shell of the vibrant, gutsy young women she once was. She was no longer a kid.

"Eve, Eve, Eve!"

Her eyes finally focused on his.

"All of New York wants your Broadway to continue. That's right, your Broadway."

Eve maintained her gaze.

"But," said Humph, "the evidence is mounting that it's

under threat. At least to my eyes. There's a truth behind my three murders that I can't put my finger on, but the more I think about it the more I think that there's a sinister scheme behind them."

Eve stood and walked to the kitchen. She grabbed an onion and sliced it with a vengeance. Her fingers barely escaped. She didn't even notice. Then she returned to her seat across the table from Humph.

"What can we do?"

"Do you know any union representatives?"

"No. No one."

"You belong to Actors' Equity, right?"

"Yeah, I think. Unions are not something me and the girls ever really talk about. Sure, we know when they're negotiating with the owners but there never seems to be any doubt that our contract will be signed. They always end up coming to terms. Since I've been there, we've never had a strike. I don't think we ever ask for the sky. Us dancers, we mostly keep reminding ourselves that these jobs are better than waitressing and a lot more fun."

Humph then explained the kind of information he was looking for, some proof that one or several of the unions was behaving out of character.

"Explain, Dad."

"Let's say by just going through the motions of bargaining. Then they come back to you and the other union members and present a new contract that is not even as good as the last one. Yet they agreed to it. If they're doing that, it's a sure sign their negotiators are working for someone other than you."

"I don't understand," said Eve.

Humph checked his pocket watch.

"God, look at the hour. I haven't had a drink all day and it's nearly midnight."

Eve said she would like a refill.

After downing a healthy sip, Humph sat back in thought for a good minute.

"OK, Eve, most shows on Broadway lose money. It's a tough business for investors. Let's say the people who have backed your show... How long has it been now that people have been working on it?"

"More than a year," Eve answered.

"OK, what if the costs have been piling up for more than a year at a far greater rate than the money guys expected. The show isn't even ready for Broadway yet and they're panicking. Even if it turns out to be a critical success, what if the money runs out five or six months down the road before anyone has made a profit. Remember, not only do they have to pay your salaries, they have to pay a huge rent to the theater owner. They have to pay all the theater's expenses, in other words everyone who works there, from ushers to the girl who sells tickets."

Eve said she'd never looked at it that way. Humph nodded and continued.

"Now, let's say a mob member has found some leverage to take control of a particular union. Let's say they discovered that the union president has been cheating on his wife. The mob doesn't just say, 'Tsk, tsk.' It suggests their silence has a price, namely that the mob will tell him how much to ask for in the coming negotiations. They might even agree beforehand to a rollback of wages as a demonstration of their goodwill toward the owners and a shared desire to keep the show going. If any of the members disagree, the mob says they would have no trouble finding scabs to replace them.

"I'm just making this up as I go, Eve, but the mob has a long history of infiltrating unions."

"I still don't get it," said Eve. "They end up lowering the wages of union members. The investors end up with silly smiles on their faces and slightly lower expenses. But what does the mob get?"

Humph smiled.

"That's my girl!"

Eve had asked the question he hoped she'd ask. The answer to it would reveal the plot to assault Broadway.

"Do you like serial movies, Eve, you know the ones you have to keep returning to the movie theater every Saturday to see the next chapter in the story?"

"Love them."

"We'll you're living in one right now. You're going to have to return next Saturday for the answer to your question: What does the mob get?"

"You can't throw me out now!"

"I am. I have to see Detective Higgins tomorrow to test some of my theories before I tell you more. In the meantime, just do what I told you before. Talk to as many people as you can. Hopefully someone will be suspicious and have some kind of insider information about one of your unions starting to act in unexpected ways as the new negotiations approach."

"Thanks, Dad. But I really just came here to ask if you had a sleeping potion of any kind. Now, thanks to you, I'll likely see the sun rise."

CHAPTER 19

WHEN Humph arrived at the stationhouse the next morning to see Detective Higgins, he was almost bowled over by a covey of cops manhandling three men toward holding cells.

When he got to the second floor, Higgins was on the phone, uncharacteristically ripping a strip off somebody at the other end of the line.

"Having a spat with your wife, Henry?"

"Heaven forbid," the detective said, slamming down the phone. "No, I was yelling at the chief of D's in Brooklyn. I'd called him about your man of the month, that Gagliardi fellow. I asked him to ask his boys if they knew him and whether they suspected him of having mob ties."

"Of course," said Humph. "Gagliardi's a Brooklyn boy."

"Well, Humph, the mere suggestion that he might be up to no good set the inspector off. You'd think I'd insulted his mother for Christ's sake. I let him run out of steam and then I pounced."

"What do you make of it?"

"Obviously, there's no reason for a chief of detectives to be offended by a request for information from another detective. I asked him whether this guy was mob connected. That's when he blew up."

"Cover-up," said Humph.

"I smell the same thing," said Higgins.

Humph reminded Higgins that he'd come to see him to get an answer to that very question.

"I'm guessing you didn't strike gold in Brooklyn."

"Not yet, Humph. But I'll get my guys to make inquiries of cops they know on that side of the bridge. Give me a minute or two."

He left the detective office and went downstairs. In about 10 minutes he returned with three constables and a sergeant.

"What is it that they call the Dodgers?" Higgins asked.

"Bums."

"Right, these guys are my Brooklyn bums, but let me tell you, they do win more than the public gives them credit for."

Humph liked baseball, although he was a Giants fan. He appreciated Higgins' introduction, as smooth as a 4-6-3 double play.

Higgins addressed the cops he'd brought in.

"Humph here spent time with the president of the Broadway League, the guys who run the show, so to speak. Humph asked him about the Broadway unions. There are tons of them. Humph wanted to know if there had been any signs the mob was trying to muscle in on the current negotiations."

Humph picked up where Higgins left off.

"First of all, the League president hadn't been made aware of anything suspicious. Secondly, he hadn't heard of the Gagliardi fellow. And thirdly, he doubted the mob could influence the unions, who had always had a harmonious relationship with the theaters and investors."

Humph shifted his chair to face the coppers directly.

"The president concluded this despite having been told that a few years ago, at a conference of the most powerful mob leaders in the country, there was talk about infiltrating Broadway just as they had already done in Hollywood."

Humph explained who Gagliardi was and admitted he didn't have any hard facts on the guy tying him to the mob. But he lived in Brooklyn and had already tried taking over a theater.

"I got the Broadway association to give me a list of all their unions and names of their leaders. I'm hoping some people I know on Broadway can unearth some information about the latest negotiations or union troubles but you're the guys who know how to investigate them. So, for now, we need a two-pronged attack, the unions and Gagliardi."

After turning his chair to face Higgins again, Humph turned to the cops to add that he also had Duffy on the Gagliardi case.

"In that case, Gagliardi's already done for," laughed one of the cops. "How's the Duffer doing?" asked another.

Higgins raised his hand and called for attention.

"Before you guys leave for your liquid lunch, I'm going to tell you a little bit about how the mob infiltrates unions, here and in Hollywood. I worked out there, remember? You'll need to know what signs to look for. And as for you Humph, I'm sorry I couldn't provide you with what you expected this morning. Let me say you laid the table for my boys just the way I would have. Say hi to Duffy for me."

Humph had no leads of his own at the moment. He walked out of the station and went straight home. There was no point in going to Duffy's. He was either sleeping one off or he was over in Brooklyn sticking his nose in unwanted places.

Later that afternoon, he got a call from Duffy.

"What a job, Humph. You work from home. Nap when you want. You tell yourself brain work is as important as pounding the pavement. The Life of Reilly, I tell you. I should call you Mr. Reilly from now on, just like the old song."

"Are you quite finished, Duff?"

"You know me, Humph. I'm never finished."

"Talk. What has all your dreary pavement pounding uncovered?"

Duffy said he didn't go straight to Brooklyn as Humph had requested because the Irishman had a truck load of connections there. He made a beeline for Broadway.

"If fact, I introduced myself to the lovely ladies and gents at your girl's show. Eve herself helped me with the introductions. In fact, I must point out, Humph, that she seemed unsure of what to call me."

"Duffy, I frequently don't know what to call you."

"Screw you, big guy. Anyway, if I may continue, I heard a couple of stagehands mention hush-hush-like that one of the union reps was putting on airs. He represented a Broadway union called IATSE. It sounds like an itchy skin rash if you ask me. They represent a ton of crafts. They're an old union, maybe the first on Broadway. Anyway, the people I talked to said this union rep was saying they shouldn't jump right in and sign anything. He never said why. They said in the past no one had ever said they should jump right in and sign, sign, sign. So, they wondered, why was this guy, someone they all had known from previous contracts, telling them to put on the brakes with this coming contract?

"That's as far as I got. However, guess who is in that union, Humph. None other than the beautiful Rebecca, make-up artist to the stars and friend of lowly flatfoots."

Duffy said that Humph might want to be the one to talk to her.

Part of Humph wished she weren't involved but another part wanted to see her. Furthermore, he told himself, she had principles and a sense of right and wrong, witness the forceful Tompkins Square evictions.

"Definitely, Duffy. Thanks for giving me the option."

Duffy then announced he was heading down into the subway at 42nd Street.

"Brooklyn bound, laddy."

Humph phoned Rebecca. No answer.

On one hand, Humph was happy his theory of a mob takeover of Broadway was starting to appear less and less absurd but he realized they'd only found crumbs of potential evidence.

He tried calling Rebecca several times throughout the afternoon and early evening. Still no answer.

He poured himself a drink and opened his library copy of *Brave New World*. What a dark picture of life, he thought, yet the idea of Broadway being overrun by mobsters seemed to spell the same kind of doom. Despite not having paid a lot of attention to Broadway until Eve began working there, he had quickly seen a kind of magic in it, one that Depression-hobbled New Yorkers needed.

Sometime after 10 p.m., he dozed off with the book on his lap.

When the doorbell rang, he grabbed the book with both hands for some reason. It took him a moment to realize someone was at the door.

Rebecca wore no make-up. Her face was bruised and cut. She had met a world she'd never known before except for stories in the papers.

Humph put his arm around her shoulders and held her right hand as he led her to the bed. He propped up several pillows with his other hand and lifted her onto the bed, positioning her in a half-seated position. Still holding her hand, he sat next to her. He saw more bruises on her upper arm, as if she'd been grabbed hard and perhaps thrown.

Seeing that Humph was putting two and two together, she blurted out that two supposed union members had kidnapped her after the union meeting. They took her to a reeking rooming house and punched her over and over again.

"One twisted my arm while the other punched me. They stopped only when I said I had no more questions to ask at meetings."

Tears seeped from her eyes. She was the kind of woman Humph had trouble imagining in tears. She was a fighter in life. She made an important place for herself on Broadway despite being Puerto Rican and Black. Eve had told him once that Rebecca was loved and respected for her talent. Eve said Broadway had its problems with race but most of the people who comprised a show, from actors to stagehands, adored talent wherever it was found.

"A bunch of them, all White, even went with her to help her get her place on Avenue B," Eve said. "They gave her references."

Not quite knowing what to do, Humph rose. He went to the kitchen and put on a pot of coffee. He also poured a drink for Rebecca. When he returned to her side, he offered her a choice. She took the drink.

After taking a sip, she clutched Humph's hand.

"They're moving fast," she said through swollen lips.

"Who?"

"The people you talked about, the ones who are taking over the union. For some reason, our union president has remained silent. In fact, Humph, we never see him even at union meetings. No one says his name. When we ask these newcomers about him, they say he had a prior engagement or crap like that."

Humph thought for several minutes, still letting

Rebecca clutch his hand.

"Are they trying to deliver some kind of message to you and the other members?"

Rebecca nodded painfully.

"What is that message? Just the essence of it if you can put it into words?"

After a few seconds, Rebecca released his hand and closed her eyes. Before she opened them again, she blindly reached out for his hand. She grabbed his muscled forearm instead.

"We'll talk in the morning, Rebecca. Sleep if you can. I'll be right here."

Humph released her hand and pulled up the cover.

He went to the kitchen table and had another drink. How to proceed? Even if it was clear to members that someone was trying to take over a union, how do you prosecute? What do you arrest them for?"

After his second Scotch, he realized the only way was to either get testimony from a union victim of some kind, like the head of Rebecca's union, that he was being blackmailed or coerced against his will or get proof that the guy moving in on them was connected to a criminal gang of some kind. That wasn't as easy as it sounded. Humph knew that from experience.

He needed to talk to both Duffy and Higgins again. He prayed the beating Rebecca took would set a fire under them.

Humph finally called it quits. He gently slipped into bed beside Rebecca. He didn't undress. He was happy it was fall, not summer.

He dreamed of a chapter in *Brave New World*. Humph rarely dreamed of sex. But he woke up in the middle of the night realizing he'd dreamed of a scene in the book. He got out of bed and looked it up. In it, members of society take part in a group sexual encounter called the Solidarity Service Orgy. The idea behind the event was apparently to encourage a sense of unity and eliminate possessiveness or jealousy among the participants. In the weird way that dreams disguise facts and truths, Humph's groggy recollection of his dream transposed the orgy to Broadway unions. While still rubbing sleep out of his eyes, Humph instantly understood that to mean that some force was trying to make union members think alike about something, like a confrontation with the Broadway League in negotiations. It was only later the next day that he realized the dream could simply have reflected the fact he was sharing his bed with a beautiful, brave woman who clearly liked and trusted him. Humph knew he was tortoise-like in realizing things like that. Eve had told him so.

Duffy came by around mid-morning. One look at Rebecca made him suggest firmly that she should see a doctor. Rebecca declined. Sober, Duffy could be argued with. Rebecca won.

Humph had also called Eve, telling her to pick up ice along the way and petroleum jelly to treat the contusions.

"What the hell is petroleum jelly?" Duffy asked skeptically.

"A mixture of oils and waxes. People swear by it. If it makes you feel any better, Duff, know that it was invented across the way in Brooklyn."

Duffy said he was still at the stage of getting to know the players in the Broadway unions and the theater owners as well.

"Had no bloody idea things had gone so far that union members were being beaten and threatened," said Duffy.

"Me neither," Humph agreed. "Once Eve gets here to treat Rebecca, we should track down Det. Higgins to see if his boys have come up with anything on Gagliardi."

"Screw that. That's what your blower is for. May the saints preserve shoe leather." Then Duffy added:

"I'll do the talking. Not that you ain't a copper until

your dying day but I suspect I can inspire Higgins's lads better than you."

The phone call lasted only a minute.

"Higgy ordered me to get down to his office tooty sweety. Who does he think he is?"

"I'd say, I think he thinks he's chief of detectives," answered Humph with a smile.

Duffy left immediately, not out of obedience but, though he wouldn't admit it, the sight of Rebecca's bruises and cuts offended something deep down inside of him. He wanted answers. He wanted culprits.

After he left, Rebecca asked for a drink. As Humph was preparing one, she asked if his phonograph worked.

On a table at the foot of the bed was a portable phonograph in a brown box. It was new, a gift from a former client in the music business. He had few records. He sat on the edge of the bed with the recordings in his hands. He read out the titles. When he got to the hit song of that year, *Stormy Weather,* Rebecca pounded the mattress and nodded. Speaking was still painful. A minute later Ethel Waters' voice filled the apartment.

Humph watched as she listened with her eyes closed. It seemed she was trying to move her lips to the lyrics. When the song finished, she asked Humph to play it one more time.

Her next request was *Body & Soul,* which hit Tin Pan Alley only three years earlier. Musicians, the ones who soloed, loved the two key changes. Humph wasn't sure what vocalists thought about them. Humph had loved music since childhood but claimed he couldn't sing a note. As a teenager, he imagined playing trumpet. Sometimes he felt that would put him too much center stage, too much in the limelight. A buddy, who played kazoo, told him his big hands should be prowling the neck of a bass. That's the way he put it, "prowling". Humph liked that.

Before *Body & Soul* finished, Rebecca had dozed off

again, her drink untouched.

Eve arrived not long after.

"How long has she been asleep?"

"Five, 10 minutes."

Eve sat next to Rebecca.

"God damn it. All she did was tell this hot shot, who claimed he represented our union president, to put a sock in it until our guy returns."

Humph asked whether she saw the beating.

"No but when the rest of us started yelling the same thing Rebecca said to him, he disappeared out the door and brought in two goons. They all but carried Rebecca out. She's a sweet girl but my God can she curse."

"And the beating?"

"Right outside the door. We all heard it. I heard a voice yell, "Girlie, things are changing. The faster you accept it the healthier you'll be!"

"We couldn't get out to help. Someone must have been leaning against the door."

Rebecca started to wake up as Eve placed the cold compress against her upper lip. Eve paused and lifted Rebecca's head onto her lap. Rebecca's eyes opened and recognized her Broadway friend. She couldn't smile.

"You gotta do something, Dad!"

Humph heard but didn't reply to the obvious. He was pacing up and down the length of the tiny apartment.

"I've got to step out. This place is too small. I need room to think."

Once outside he walked two blocks west, then crossed the street and headed back. Before arriving at his place, he stopped at the newsstand he went to every morning.

"Missed you this morning, Humph," said the vender.

"Yeah. Unexpected crap. It's piling up. Give me a paper anyway."

Without looking at the paper, Humph went to the

payphone behind the newsstand. He called his friend Gerald Franklin at the *New York World*. Humph had learned that newspaper guys sometimes lucked into information they didn't realize was important. If you keep your nose in other people's business long enough, you'll smell a rat of some kind.

Humph was kept waiting for five minutes. He wasn't in the mood to wait. A case had become personal. Ordinarily, he would try to withdraw from it. This time, no. Not with Rebecca involved, and, he had to admit, Eve in equal measure.

Finally Gerald came on the line.

Humph bowled over the pleasantries.

"What do you know about mob involvement in Broadway? And more specifically, what do you know about a pushy pretender named Walton Gagliardi?"

Gerald was taken aback by Humph's assault. It wasn't like him.

"Can I call you back in half an hour, Humph? I need to poke around some files and talk to a couple of the boys."

When Franklin called back, Humph had calmed down. He was no longer expecting good news. He knew for certain now that he was more attracted to Rebecca than he wanted to admit. His love life hadn't been the greatest. He'd lost the great love of his life years before and had avoided women for years afterwards. Then he fell for a wonderful woman who also happened to be a cop in the NYPD's Women's League. Despite himself, he'd had big hopes but like the woman in question, he came to the same conclusion after a passion-propelled journey to Miami that died like fruit on the vine when they realized that when they were away from the life in the department they had too little in common.

Humph was now the detective he'd always been.

"For starters, Humph, we have a file on this guy. He was nailed 11 years ago for running a whore house with six girls no older than 17. He got off when the judge suddenly had a heart attack and his replacement found that the girls were sadly homeless waifs and that Mr. Gagliardi had done the Christian thing in offering them protection from the evils of society."

Humph kept silent. He was all too familiar with the city's profoundly irrational judiciary. He often classified the judiciary as criminal, or at least judicially inept.

"Of course, my friend, the whole case stank to high heaven. We even wrote an editorial demanding a new trial and a new judge. But it was to no avail. In case you didn't know, there's another judge who sells young boys, teenagers, to the highest bidder. The kids have committed felonies and they are told they have to choose between jail and sexual servitude. They choose the latter because they figure they won't get a record and that they might be able to escape. They have no idea what awaits them. High society has long and ugly claws to hold them in place."

It took Humph a minute to digest this new background for Gagliardi. Obviously, he was a bad guy with connections. How could he have those connections, with judges and high society, without being affiliated with the mob? Simple answer: he couldn't.

"Do we know which mob guys he's connected to?"

"Our files don't mention anybody. But hold on, Humph, if you want us to start excavating his past, you got to dangle a story in front of me. What do we get in return?"

Humph's head was swimming. He was delighted he had proof that Gagliardi was at the least a criminal and at worst a made member of the mob who could get protection from the highest levels of the judiciary and society. His investigation, the NYPD's investigation, now had a clear target. However, how could they stop the infiltration of the Broadway unions? How long were Gagliardi's tentacles?"

An hour later, Duffy rang.

"I'll be there in 20 minutes." He didn't wait for Humph

to reply before hanging up.

While waiting, Humph refreshed Eve's drink. Rebecca's head was now on her lap. Eve gently ran her fingers through the thick black strands. Humph raised the drink to her lips.

With a bang, Duffy barged through the door. You can't teach a bulldog new tricks, Humph thought.

Duffy quickly took in Eve bringing Rebecca slowly back to life. He took Humph's upper arm and all but dragged the big man to the window. They looked down to the street as Duffy began his account of the meeting with Higgins.

"Higgy was like a heaven-sent testifier, Humph. Not only did he acknowledge Gagliardi's evident mob connection, he said Gagliardi's first name, at birth, was not Walton but Arturo. His parents said *addio* to this world when he was 13. Some kind of boating accident in Central Park. How you overturn a rowboat I don't know. Anyway, they both drowned. At the age of 16, our enterprising lad had his name changed legally and started presenting off-the-wall business ideas to small Brooklyn companies. He figured he'd get a better reception with a touch of English ancestry. Personally, I can't see why he would bother doing that in Brooklyn of all places."

Humph pointed his index finger at Duffy and traced rapid circles with it. "Speed it up."

Humph's stage directions didn't work. Over the next 15 minutes, he learned who Arturo dated, where he worked, where he got fired, where he got the crap beat out of him, and, at long last, where he encountered local mobsters.

"Long story short, Humph…"

"Thank God," Humph said. "Your tenacious diligence is worth many an Irish whiskey, Duff, but my patience is on, to understate things, an impossibly short leash."

Duffy smiled. "Do you actually have Irish whiskey or are you just saying, like…?"

Humph affected a glare. Duffy resumed.

"Our friend Arturo got his baptism in garbage, so

to speak. Following mob instructions, he turned a large Brooklyn garbage truck operation into a personal cash fund, from which he dutifully provided a share to his mob mentors. His basic strategy was to suddenly announce huge increases in pick-up costs. The union didn't see a cent but drivers enjoyed dumping garbage in front of places, homes and businesses, that didn't want to pay the increase."

Then jumping to the present, Duffy said the that the president of Eve's and Rebecca's union was easily convinced to keep his mouth shut about who was really running the union. Apparently he was enamored of two teenage boys from the old neighborhood. The mob had him by the short and curlies."

"So," interrupted Humph, "our boy knows how to take over a union."

"Without the slightest doubt," said Duffy. "I can give you other, more sophisticated examples of union takeovers. There were enough of them that his mob bosses made him. As far as the mob was concerned, Arturo had proven he could bring in money. He was now a made man, a man of honor, as the mob would say. Future guaranteed, if that can be said of anyone in the mob."

"So, Duffy, what about his attempted intervention in Harlem, that Latino dance joint?"

"Well Humph, the amazing Higgy was on top of that, too. The approach that you heard about, you know, when Arturo approached the owners and got turned down flat, that turns out to be just a polite overture. Two months later, the mob paid off the club's substantial bank loan, and presented the owners with a bill requiring immediate repayment. Of course, the club couldn't afford to do that. Arturo's people drew up a payment plan that included signing off on mob ownership of 51% of the club. The club is basically Arturo's. He can dance salsa any night he wants with no cover charge."

Humph patted Duffy on the back. As always, Duffy winced.

They walked from the window back to the table. Rebecca was now sitting up on the bed. Eve still had her arm around her.

Humph, to Duffy's surprise and delight, did have a virgin bottle of Irish whiskey. He placed it on the table and told Duffy to help himself. He let Duffy indulge for 10 minutes. While doing so, he sat on the bed and held Eve's hand.

When he stood again, he looked at his copper buddy and said, "All we need now is to connect Arturo or his boys to one, two or all three Broadway murders. And to do that, we have to prove he is trying to take control of the Broadway League's unions. We already know, thanks to Eve and Rebecca, that the heads of two unions are behaving out of character all of a sudden. We have link this to Arturo.

Humph told Duffy that there were several more unions who negotiated with Broadway owners every contract. He said that in the three years that the League has existed, the two sides have reached agreement without ever raising a voice. Business and labor have never gotten along so well.

Duffy poured himself another drink and announced that Higgins said his boys were about to interview each of the union honchos shortly. He pointed to the girls sitting on the edge of the bed and added, "Their inside information was good enough proof for him."

Humph turned to Eve.

"Bravo. We're on the right track, thanks to you two. When you go back to work, I don't want you taking any risks. Just be two pairs of ears to whatever information might come your way. Do not go looking for it. Do you understand?" It was more of a command than a question.

Eve nodded in the affirmative but Humph knew that didn't mean doodley squat, or as some young people were saying, diddley squat.

CHAPTER 20

THE next morning Humph stopped at the newsstand on Henry Street. The headlines of the papers that were visible under the lead bar that stopped them from flying away, or those hanging from clothes pins across the top of the stand, all proclaimed similar versions of the most gruesome headline: "Trio Chopped and Diced in Bklyn Mob Hit." At first Humph thought it meant the mob was making Chinese food. Then it sunk into his half-awake mind that "chopped" was a reference to "chopper", the slang for machine guns, and "diced" likely meant the bodies were torn to pieces by the bullets.

As for the perpetrators, the mob, they were the very people he was after for the Broadway murders. He was suddenly wide awake. In all his years in the NYPD, he never knowingly found himself in a showdown with the mob. He mostly worked Harlem as a rookie, then the Lower East Side where several of the mob's most illustrious representatives reigned supreme, Bugsy Siegel and Myer Lansky, to name just two. Humph knew their history. At one time, their gang was known as the Bugs & Myer gang, one of the mob's most violent. But Humph never dealt with them as a cop. But as a kid he knew you couldn't pinch an apple without their permission or from some kid representing them. But the gang scene in Brooklyn was more rambunctious. As someone once told him, "On that side of the bridge you grow up either wanting to be a cop or a gangster. There's no in-between except the priesthood."

When he left his apartment, his plan was to see Higgins straight away. He wanted to at least bear witness to their questioning of union members and reps on Broadway. However, he hadn't gotten far when he decided to visit Rebecca. She was probably still shaken. It would be quite a hike to Avenue B and Tompkins Square so he found a pay phone to make sure she was home.

She was.

To his surprise, she sounded full of life, the way she always did when her world was purely Broadway and not the brutal world Broadway helped thousands escape from for a few hours. Rebecca said she was going to work at noon and didn't know how late she was.

"Theater doesn't know what a clock is," she said, laughing.

Humph was hugely relieved. "I'll call," he said.

His day would be with Higgins instead of a beautiful woman.

Humph stopped along the way to the police station to have breakfast and read the papers. It turned out that the shoot-up had nothing to do with unions and labor disputes. It seemed to involve a failure to pay protection money on Flatbush Avenue. The mob must have been trying to send a message because one shopkeeper's delinquent payment hardly warranted a fusillade of lead.

At the precinct station, everything seemed strangely peaceful. Ordinarily, even if the first floor was not full to bursting with the fine citizens of New York being manhandled to the desk sergeant's throne for booking, or a cluster of unfortunates being propelled to the holding cells, there was always a buzz of amalgamated protests and sarcastic importuning by cops to move along. Today there was hardly a peep.

Before mounting the stairs to the detective's floor, Humph paused before the desk sergeant.

"Something seems amiss."

"Do you hear me complaining?" said the desk sergeant.

Humph smiled and threw him a sloppy salute before heading for the stairs. He wasn't even middle-aged but he felt gravity ridiculing him as he climbed.

Higgins was in conference with someone Humph didn't recognize. Humph did an about-face and saw an old buddy from his constabulary days.

"What's the deal downstairs?" Humph asked.

"Hello to you, too," said his old beat companion.

"Forgive me but is this a day off for crime?"

The cop laughed.

"Some asshole managed somehow to start a fire in the holding cells last night. I heard he used his own jacket and a match or two to get it going. Another guy volunteered his jacket as well. Once they got the blaze goin' good, they started screaming 'Fire! Fire!" and calling for help. Before anyone knew it, smoke was billowing through the reception area. The sergeant was screaming blue murder. I heard they called the fire department but before they arrived someone was level-headed enough to get a couple of buckets of water to put it out. However, he didn't think of bringing the keys for the cells. He used a fire ax to smash them open so he could get in with the water. The prisoners were hacking away but no one was actually burned. One wall was

WAYNE CLARK | Busted on Broadway

scorched pretty bad. Anyway, they had to be transferred to another stationhouse because two of the cells couldn't be locked anymore. The new doors arrived this morning."

Humph stared at him.

"What did they think setting fire to the cells would accomplish, other than burning themselves to a crisp?"

"Someone asked them that very question, Humph. One of them said he hoped the fire would fill the station with smoke and they'd be able to sneak out in all the confusion. Apparently the cop who broke the locks had shoulders as wide as Broad Street and none of them could squeeze by him. In fact—this is funny, Humph—once the cop had emptied the first bucket of water on the flames, he turned it over and plunked it hard on the head of the prisoner making most of the noise."

Humph smiled. The tale almost made him miss working there.

When he turned around, he saw that calm had returned to Detective Higgins's universe.

"Don't ask," Higgins ordered when Humph arrived at his desk.

"I wouldn't think of it."

Humph pulled up a chair.

"I'm told that our mysterious Mister Gagliardi is no longer mysterious."

Higgins nodded.

"Made man. A full-blown mobster who makes a point of popping up in unexpected places..."

Humph finished the sentence:

"From Latino dance halls to Broadway union meetings."

"You got it. We're still questioning every Broadway union rep we can find. I had no idea there were so many crafts and businesses involved in putting on a show, and they all seem to be unionized, from costume-makers to make-up artists like your friend, or Eve's friend, whatever.

What makes it hard to unravel is that the costume makers, who, as I said, are unionized, of course buy their cloth from shops in the garment district. The mob has a steel grip on the whole garment district. They even control the truckers who deliver the garments. So we've got a union for the seamstresses, a union for the truckers, a union for the costume makers, a union for the people who design the costumes. Don't get me started on the unions involved in set making."

Higgins said that when Humph first suggested the mob wanted to "get into show business" he was doubtful. Now, he said, he saw the opportunities galore on Broadway just ripe for the picking by the gangsters.

"Educate me," Humph said. "Explain to me how they could take over unions. I hear over and over again that the Broadway League is tickled pink. I mean the owners and other investors. And the unions are happy, too, because up until now, at least, their contract requests have all been granted."

Higgins took several moments before answering. He was inclined to lecturing but he somehow sensed there was no point in lecturing Humph. Repeatedly, the big PI had shown himself to be more intelligent than people normally give big lugs credit for. He also clearly had a detective's nose. It was unfortunate that he hadn't made detective before turning his back on the force.

"As you know, Humph, the mob takes control of unions by exploiting any weakness they have, such as a corrupt union president, one who treats union funds as his private bank, or even offering mob help to union members who want to oust their leader. Throughout New York, the mob has shown itself to be extremely deft at seducing the union guys who count. They now run trucking, and that includes garbage collection. As I mentioned. the whole garment district, which produces more than 90 percent of the clothes Americans buy. The mob has nightclubs, big, important ones, in their stable. Add to that prostitution, casinos, bootlegging, et cetera, et cetera."

Humph nodded, knowingly.

"And we know taking over Broadway isn't a big step for an outfit that already has Hollywood under its thumb. I just wanted to hear it from you. What I know is just information I got from reading mostly. I have no personal experience with the mob. You have. What's next?"

Higgins said it was important to let his boys continue nosing around the Broadway unions to see which have been approached by outsiders promising union heaven. Then we'll trying to nail down those bastards."

Before Higgins could finish, Humph said there were three murders of actors that needed to be solved.

"Surely those deaths are somewhat connected."

"Instinct tells me you're right, Humph, but I need to find the tell-tale breadcrumbs before I can act."

In the meantime, Humph said, he would go back and re-interview everyone connected with the murders. This time he would do it from the perspective of mob involvement, something that had never occurred to him at the outset.

"A two-prong investigation," said Higgins. "I've perhaps said this before but you're a man after my own heart. I'll let you know as soon as I've got anything, no matter how small. Please do the same."

Humph rose from his chair and nodded.

To his surprise, when he got downstairs, he could detect a faint smell of smoke. When he arrived at the stationhouse his mind must have been so immersed in the case that his olfactory senses were on vacation.

He phoned Rebecca from the police station. No answer. She must have been at work. He wanted to enlist her to accompany him while interviewing those connected with the killing of the three actors. She had served him well in the Harlem investigation.

Humph was too excited to go home. Where to go? Then he remembered a silly drunken comment by his friend:

"When in doubt, Duff's your do-guy."

Humph flipped a coin. Duff won.

On the top steps leading to his apartment, with scores of people within hearing distance, with hand over heart, Duffy proclaimed:

"Which of the virgin saints, none of them Irish for sure, pointed the much-heralded Humphster to my abode?"

Humph's immediate thought was: "There goes the afternoon. He's smashed."

Once inside, Duffy suddenly sounded as sober as a priest suddenly confronted by a bishop.

"I'm being watched, Humph. Seriously watched."

"By whom?"

"I'm not sure but my cop instincts have never failed me. It has to be connected with my chitty-chats at Eve's show, backstage and all that, you know."

Humph wanted to know who he suspected, did he have a name, a record, anything that would let them zero in on a mob infiltrator.

Humph couldn't remember ever seeing Duffy look as abashed as he did now.

"But you know what he looks like, right? Have you followed him."

Duffy shook his head.

"It was just yesterday that he started trying to stare me down and everyone else. One of the chorus girls was really upset by this stranger on the set and I had to comfort her."

"For Christ's sake, Duff. Screw the chorus girl in a case like that."

"Well, Humph, that's kinda what I wanted to do."

Humph stood.

"It seems that when you're sober I'm wasting my time talking to you."

"That's a tad harsh, partner."

"Pour yourself a damn big whiskey, Duff."

Duffy sat Humph down and spoke while standing in front of him, looking down on him, which was rarely possible.

"Have an imbibement yourself, old friend. You need to listen."

"Imbibement? Really, Duff? You've outdone yourself."

Regardless, Humph reached over the sofa to the table behind, lined with empty bottles and two unopened Irish whiskey bottles.

"The guy, the one who was talking up the girlies on the set said he was from… Hold on Humph. I have to check my notes. The union name is ludicrous. It's one I mentioned to you not long ago. OK, OK, here it is."

Duffy read from a shabby notebook.

"The girlies I talked to, dancers and actresses and actors, belong to something called, I'll spell it, I.A.T.S.E. I tell you, no one will ever write a love song to I.A.T.S.E. I was told it stands for the International Alliance of Theatrical Stage Employees. Apparently it was the first Broadway union. Anyway, even though most of the girls can't tell you what those initials stand for, they belong to it."

"So what?" asked Humph.

"The 'what' you so rudely asked about is that the guy hanging around asking questions about their union didn't even know the full name of the union. None of the girls had ever seen him before. And after he notices me hanging around, he follows me home. How much is two and two, Humph?"

Humph asked if the guy was still outside. Duff held up his hand, making a gesture to wait. He sauntered downstairs as if looking only to take in some of the afternoon sunshine. He sat and lit a cigarette. A few minutes later he doffed his crumpled hat to two ladies who apparently knew him. All the better for making his appearance on the stairs seem innocent. Not long after, Humph, looking through the partially drawn blinds, saw a man get out of the suspect car. He was patiently waiting for traffic to pass by, then slowly crossed the street. He casually looked right and left, then walked up to Duffy's stoop.

Duffy's window was open but Humph couldn't hear a word. However, he could see Duffy smile and offer the stranger the spot next to him on the stoop.

Humph adjusted his position on the sofa so he could see the stoop without craning his neck to the right. From the left side, he figured he could see everything. Once he made the move and pulled back the curtain, he saw the scene had changed. Duffy, still seated, held the guy in a firm headlock. The guy's legs squirmed but Duffy appeared to squeeze even tighter until the gyrations stopped. There was a feeble fluttering of the guy's hands. He wasn't dead. Thank goodness, thought Humph. He needed information.

By the time Duffy finally tugged the guy up the stairs and into his apartment, Humph was feeling strangely impatient to leave. Finally he realized that what he wanted was to bring Rebecca to Duffy's place. He wanted to put his knee on the man's chest and make him stare at Rebecca. He wanted him to say why he hit her. He grew angrier by the moment. Duff noticed.

"Whoa. Whoa, buddy."

He said they had all night to grill him.

Humph came to his senses.

"I'll be back," he said and left.

I took Humph almost three hours to track down Rebecca and bring her to Duffy's Bowery Street flat.

When they let themselves in, they found Duffy seated on the floor leaning back against an easy chair. At his feet, in fact under his outstretched legs, was the suspected mob influencer. Duffy, who had never been west of Hackensack, had tied him up like a hog at a Wild West rodeo.

"Where did you learn to do that?"

"God bless Hollywood movies. What I would love to do for my encore is ride a horse up Broadway, dressed in my finest Irish greenery. I can guarantee you that intersection coppers will stop traffic for me all the way up to Central Park."

Humph had given up trying to figure out whether Duffy was a lost cause or just acting.

"Duffy. You have a visitor, much prettier than the one you hogtied."

Duffy squinted at her. The squinting wasn't faked. He'd drunk his way off to the sunset, where any good cowboy would go. Unfortunately, here, the sun set on slums and saloons. There were stables here and there in Manhattan but Humph knew that Duffy was fantasizing about riding off into the mountains as he'd seen in movies.

"What am I supposed to do, Humph?" Rebecca asked. "Do I recognize this guy? Is that what you want to know?"

"Yes," said Humph in a soft voice. Then, speaking louder, he said:

"Cowpoke Duffy, kindly remove that stinking sock from our captive's mouth."

The whiskey had left Duffy's hands ham-fisted. The hogtied goon squealed for all he was worth. Finally, Rebecca knelt down and waved Duffy away. Within seconds, her deft hands had freed the bad guy's yapper hole, as Duffy was later to recount.

One his mouth was free, the man bellowed:

"Do you know who the fuck I am?"

Before Humph could respond, Duffy said:

"No damn idea, lad, and watch your fucking language in the presence of a lady."

Rebecca couldn't resist a chuckle at Duffy's messed-up attempt at decorum. She glanced at Humph and saw that he felt the same.

The guy then said:

"Do you know who I represent?"

Humph leapt in before Duffy could dismiss the

comment with a profanity.

"We have a very good idea. And your connection with that person is not going to bode well for you in court."

Rebecca interrupted to say that this was definitely the guy who told the costumers' union that their president was a pervert and had to be removed. He said that he would be their new president. He said he was just an interim president until the members could elect a new one. It sounded so plausible and innocent at the time. Then we found out about the rest."

"The rest?"

Even Duffy resurfaced long enough to say the same words.

"Yes, Humph. He told us that we would have to accept a reduction in salary. He said the Depression had left Broadway on the brink of collapse. Ticket sales were way down. Investors were impossible to find. He said the Broadway League believed the only way to save Broadway was to create a budget Broadway. Apparently the plan was to stage fewer shows but they'd be ones there were backed to the hilt, publicity, the works."

A lot of that made sense. The president of the Broadway League himself had told Humph that attendance had shrunk since the start of the Depression. People simply couldn't afford the already ridiculously low prices for tickets. Tourists, Broadway's bread and butter, weren't travelling to New York anymore.

Humph asked for a time-out. He had a phone call he had to make.

He went down to the street and found a pay phone. He had no idea whether his call would even be accepted.

"Good afternoon," a pleasant woman's voice said. "This is the office of the Broadway League. How can I help you."

Humph gave his name and said it was urgent that he speak to Mr. King, the president.

"Please hold."

Humph wasn't tense because he had no reason to think his call would be put through.

After a couple of minutes, the same woman returned to the line and said that Mr. King would be available in a few minutes. "Can you hold?" Humph wanted to kiss her.

When King came on the line, Humph asked him point blank whether Broadway was going to reinvent itself as a budget Broadway.

"Absolutely not, Humph. "We've already chosen productions for next season that we hope will not require exorbitant budgets. I won't say that we've chosen scripts that appeal only to the masses but we've lowered our standards a bit. Without a healthy Broadway, there's no real New York that matters much."

That was enough for Humph. He knew King was sincere and what he said made sense.

He took a taxi back to Duffy's. It was worth the money.

When he walked into the living room, he was shocked. Rebecca sat on the floor with the head of the mobster on her lap.

Humph took in the scene, Rebecca on the floor cradling the mobster's head, Duffy still leaning against his armchair, apparently asleep.

"He mostly wanted to talk about his momma," said Rebecca, taking in Humph's piercing gaze.

Humph didn't sit. He continued to stand, staring.

"It seems," Rebecca said, "that this fellow thought we were going to kill him. At one point your Mr. Duffy stepped on his chest on the way to the bathroom. The guy was sure Duff was going to come back and stand on his chest until he died."

She added that while Duffy was in the can he told her that there were other unions under the same threat by his boss.

"He was in a lot of pain after hours of Duffy's restraints. I mean big-time pain. So I kind of believe him. He said a guy named Gagliardi was orchestrating the whole damn thing, union by union. Then he nearly passed out. When he came to he said, 'Honey, by telling you that, I am dead. Tell my momma that...' He passed out again. Here he is. Alive. Barely. I don't think he even wants to breathe again."

Humph was surprised that Rebecca could talk that calmly and professionally about death, even a mobster's.

Humph tapped Duffy's cheeks lightly. No response. He was gone. Humph then asked Rebecca to phone the cops.

"Tell them Humph and Duffy have corralled a criminal. Please pick him up. Tell them he's hogtied in our living room at the moment."

Humph knew that a clearly stated, sober request from a woman would get a quick response.

Three-quarters of an hour later, there were no bodies in Duffy's place. When he awoke, he gazed around the room and said, "I could have sworn I had a visitor."

When Humph turned around, Rebecca was standing and clearly ready to go.

Humph was so slow to respond that she finally said,

"Thanks for dragging me here for such a good time. I'll never be able to describe this day to anyone. Any more near murders you want me to witness, Humph?"

She was out the door before Humph could mutter a word.

When Humph got home, he peeled off his clothes with a vengeance and threw himself on his bed. Why, he asked himself, could he not understand women?

CHAPTER 21

THE next morning Humph was at his stubborn best. He was frustrated about Rebecca's sudden flight the night before but he was even more frustrated this morning by the fact he'd made no progress in finding motives or suspects in the seemingly nonsensical murders of three actors. Although it appeared that Rebecca would be unlikely to want to join him, his need to cross T's and dot i's made it absolutely necessary to revisit those cases, this time from the perspective of mob involvement. He had no evidence to suggest there was but that just made it even more tempting to revisit the murders.

He first called Det. Higgins to see if he had heard of the case Rebecca had alerted police to.

"You mean the mob guy who'd been nosing around the Broadway unions?"

"That's the one."

"We've got him in hospital under guard at the moment. It seems our old friend Duffy took the law into his own hands more than usual."

"That he did," said Humph. "I regret having left his place during his rather besotted interrogation. On the other hand, with the so-called victim's admission that he was mobbed up, my sympathy goes only so far."

Higgins said Duffy's excesses didn't hide the confirmation that the mob was moving in on Broadway.

"It's a bold move, if you ask me," said Humph. "You'd think the bad guys would consider Broadway a bit too public to mess around with."

Higgins said he agreed and disagreed.

"The mob isn't afraid of anyone or anything. They already control so much in this town that stretching their tentacles to the Great White Way seems right down their line. When they have to, they can finesse their operations. However, in examining their motive, there's another factor."

Like a boy in the back row of desks at school who is suddenly starts pumping his hand in the air to be asked to answer something, Humph interrupts the detective to say:

"Like everyone in this Depression, Broadway investors are losing a lot of money, more than ever apparently. What a perfect way for the mob to launder its dirty money: invest in shows that are bound to tank."

"You get a gold star for that one, Humph. A solid point. But I can do you one better. Drum roll, please."

After a sufficient pause, Higgins asked, "Besides Santa Clause, what will be coming around come December this year?"

Humph stood to think more clearly but after a moment he confessed he was stumped.

"The end of Prohibition!" The unusually undemonstrative detective was thrilled with his own thinking.

Almost in unison, the two men said:

"…and the mob will be out a fortune in illicit booze operations."

They will want to make up for that loss for sure, said the detective.

"Give their regards to Broadway," said Humph, almost singing the words.

Humph's day brightened. There was light at the end of the tunnel for the first time since he started working on this case.

"What can we pin on them now?" Humph asked.

Higgins said they could certainly arrest the gangster Duffy manhandled. But he added that his boys were probably at that very moment interviewing the union leader the mob was blackmailing.

"That should take us a legal step further and it may lead to other avenues of investigation. The more names we get the better."

"Or course," said Humph. "One last point for this morning, Henry. You said Gagliardi is clever. He has many names and personas. And he knows his way around showbiz a bit."

"Right."

Humph then told him that he wanted to revisit the three murders of actors with that bit of information in mind. Maybe, he said, someone with knowledge of those killings unknowingly encountered a mobster in disguise.

Humph needed to stretch his legs. He wasn't sure what to do next. He looked at his notes for the three murders. Nothing jumped to mind. Some exercise and breakfast might help.

Before he was a block from his apartment, he stopped at a payphone and called Rebecca.

To his surprise, the coldness of her departure the night before had disappeared. That was, he thought, further proof that he didn't understand women.

She said she wasn't working that day. Relieved, Humph

summarized the conversation and conclusions he and the detective had reached.

"Where do you want to meet," Rebecca said.

That woman, thought Humph, had a way of avoiding unnecessary words. Action time.

"Bellevue Hospital, at the gates."

Mrs. Sidwell, the bored society woman suspected of killing the young Haitian actor she adored, was still in the ward for mentally disturbed patients. It was looking like she'd remain there for the rest of her days. The last time Humph checked on her condition, he learned that her big-shot husband had not visited even once, which probably didn't disturb her in the slightest. She had made it clear to Humph during their interview at her apartment that she despised him. She said he conducted his life as if she wasn't in it.

Rebecca was waiting for him. He felt like a boy on a first date, not a PI investigating a murder. He gave Rebecca a peck on the cheek then withdrew quickly.

"So," he said. But he didn't finish the sentence.

Rebecca did.

"You already told me that you don't think this woman could possibly have killed the young man, right? But you think her muddled, love-stricken brain might have somehow picked up on clues we could use."

"Basically, that's it. I couldn't have expressed it better myself."

She smiled.

They entered the ward. A nurse led the way.

"Hello, my dear!" she said in that high-society, faux-British voice that so enervated Humph. The welcome was phonier than a vegetable steak.

However, once again she did remember him.

"And if I may ask, young man, who is that captivating lady in your company?"

Humph introduced Rebecca, describing her as a friend.

Humph then adopted Mrs. Sidwell's stilted phrasing.

"Would you mind terribly if we asked you for further recollections of the night the poor young actor died?"

"Oh, my goodness," she gushed. "Such a very long time ago, wasn't it."

"Not really, Mrs. Sidwell. Take your time. My memory plays tricks on me as well."

Rebecca, Humph could see, was hiding a smirk.

"Darling boy," she said finally. "In fact, my dreams have reacquainted me with the boy's demise."

After that she said nothing.

Humph finally asked:

"And what did your dreams reveal?"

"Not to put too fine a point on it but my dreams said I didn't lay a finger on the young man. I just assembled my dignity and walked out. You know," she said after a pause, "I've never hurt a soul in my life, as much as a may have wanted to. And, I know, young man, that you know of whom I speak."

Humph nodded his understanding. He felt much the same way about her so-called husband.

"May I ask, Mrs. Sidwell, who told you that your young actor friend was being deceitful, as it were, or to put it crudely, having dalliances with other, younger women?"

Mrs. Sidwell's eyes turned inwards for the longest time. The nurse entered with her morning tea but Mrs. Sidwell appeared not to notice.

Finally, she looked at Rebecca. There was no recognition in her face. Then she suddenly saw Humph.

"Oh, dear, there you are. I do recall something. There was a man who approached me before I even met my young man that evening. He was swarthy and quite dashing in his own way. He was the one who told me about my young actor's affairs with other, younger women. He even said I mustn't let my justifiable anger take control of me."

Her voice trailed off.

Finally she came back to the present.

"Mr. Humph, sir, only just now do I see him slipping a knife into my hand, just as he was saying I mustn't let my anger get hold of me. As sure as I can reach out and touch your hand, sir, I feel the knife slipping from my grasp. I left horrified."

She stared at Humph for at least a minute. Humph did not want to interrupt her recollection.

"Is it possible the I didn't kill the boy, that this man did, making it look like lover's quarrel? Please tell me?"

There was desperation in her voice. Humph took a photo from his pocket and showed it to her.

"Is this possibly the man who slipped a knife into your hand?"

"Yes! Yes! That's him."

It was a photo of Gagliardi.

Humph stood and kissed her forehead.

"I can't thank you enough, Mrs. Sidwell."

"Clarissa, please feel free to call me Clarissa."

As they got back to Second Avenue, Rebecca said:

"Sad."

Humph agreed but said nothing.

Next was the second murder. They went to the site of the killing, an upscale restaurant, but their queries and the photo of Gagliardi drew an absolute blank. Police had never been able to find a witness, even though several people saw a good-looking blonde woman quickly walk up to the actor's table, shoot him between the eyes, and vanish. The only way it was possible that no one could provide details about the killer was that she was elegant enough to look like she belonged in such a place and she had concealed her weapon to the very last second before pulling the trigger two feet from the actor.

Once again, the police unearthed no useful witness

accounts. No one had seen the woman before although men were able to describe her in detail. "Stunning," one restaurant patron said.

The third victim perished much the same way.

"One conclusion," said Humph at the end of an exhausting afternoon of tracking down witnesses and asking questions that drew blank looks, "They were professional hits in all cases. The dinner companions in two of the cases likely had nothing whatsoever to do with the killings."

Why would Gagliardi have them killed? Over the next two days, Humph threw that question at everyone connected with the investigation, from Eve to Det. Higgins to stagehands he met behind the curtains while visiting Eve during rehearsals. Each dead actor belonged to a different show.

It was finally Higgins who came up with a plausible theory. Gagliardi and the mob were gunning for control of as many shows as they could.

"I've called all my boys to a meeting this evening. So far they've come up with little usable information. I'm hoping this new theory, about Gagliardi casting a wide net, will raise the stakes and instill some damn urgency into the investigation. If my boys can find connections, threads, similarities, things in common about what's going on with the union memberships at several shows, we'll know we're onto something."

He added that he planned to call in a retired cop, a detective who had worked on several crackdowns on mob union busting.

Humph couldn't have asked for more but his impatience was almost unbearable. Sitting idle while Higgins directed the small army of detectives didn't suit his nature, but this time, Eve was involved.

"…and," continued Higgins, "Rebecca."

CHAPTER 22

HUMPH had resigned himself to waiting on a call from Higgins. But he couldn't resist devouring the papers for possibly related crimes, particularly mob-related ones.

On the second morning of his seclusion, the morning papers mentioned a shootout in downtown Brooklyn, on Fulton Street, one of city's oldest. All he had to do was walk a couple of blocks toward the East River and his magic carpet would take him and his impatience across the river to a crime scene that probably hadn't the slightest connection with his case or the mob. Private eyes get that way. The paper had a photo of the guy. Humph clipped it out and took it with him.

In Brooklyn, people got permanently "disappeared" for a host of reasons, from stealing their mother-in-law's purse to absconding with the seal of the city of Brooklyn. Brooklyn thieves, thought Humph, may be mostly stupid but no one can say they're not brazen.

Humph was in a flighty state. The strange thing was, he was aware of it. None of his rational friends, especially fellow coppers, would have ever acknowledged such a phenomenon. He was a Rock of Gibraltar kind of guy.

Once on Fulton Street, Humph asked around about an individual whose future got curtailed the previous night.

No one in local restaurants or bars had ever seen the victim before, or so they said. Although Humph didn't introduce himself as a private eye, a couple of the barkeeps fingered him. They extended their fingers subtly in a gimme-gimme flutter but Humph wasn't buying. As yet, he had no reason to believe the rub-out had anything to do with his case or even the mob.

Since he was already in Brooklyn, and on Fulton Street, Humph flipped a coin. Tails. That meant he had to at least be sociable to a Brooklynite. The city had become part of New York only 35 years before so few Manhattanites regarded Brooklynites as full-fledged citizens, a fact that didn't bother most Brooklynites in the slightest. It was the politicians who wanted the amalgamation of all New York's boroughs. They wanted a piece of Manhattan's monster-sized tax base to fund local projects.

During his exploration of bars and diners, he made note of the offices of the *Brooklyn Eagle Daily*. He'd heard that it was the country's largest-circulation paper, or at least was at some point. Brooklyn was always full of surprises, he thought. The paper was located down at 28 Fulton, a stone's throw away.

His buddy at the *New York World*, Gerald Franklin, had once mentioned a buddy of his, a columnist at the *Daily Eagle*. He couldn't say enough about him. This friend was a writer who couldn't spell. His first name was Rian, Rian James. Who spelled Ryan that way? The visit was a stretch for Humph but he prided himself on his thoroughness. Or was it purposeless stubbornness? The question had occurred to him but he had never dwelt on it long enough to get close to answering it.

James was in. They shook hands after Humph introduced himself as a long-time friend of Gerald Franklin. He immediately volunteered that he and "Gerry" were planning on meeting for a tipple next week.

After Humph explained that he was a private eye and former cop, James's journalistic instinct jumped into high gear and he wanted to know everything about whatever case Humph was currently working on. Humph told him as much as he could but ended up shrugging his shoulders as a sign that he and the cops in Manhattan were at a dead end despite having three Broadway murders on their hands.

James was clearly fascinated but he said he had to admit he was mostly writing about New York's best restaurants these days.

"A strange beat," he admitted, "considering that this current economic calamity denies even some well-off people the pleasure of fine dining. But people seem to want to read about make-believe life because of the Depression."

After a pause, James added:

"Wouldn't you agree, Humph? It's like the movies. People are flocking to make-believe storylines, aren't they."

Not being a movie-goer, Humph couldn't respond. After a silence that was approaching the awkward stage, Humph decided to announce that he'd done his research.

"Much like what I imagine a reporter does," he said. Switching to the columnist's first name, Humph said:

"Rian, I know about your recent success."

Rian looked befuddled.

What a good actor he was, thought Humph, full of admiration for the writer's humility.

"Gerald told me. He was so excited for you."

Rian gave in.

"So?"

What the columnist had been holding back about himself was the fact that he had just sold a screenplay to Hollywood. It wasn't just any screenplay. It would change his life forever and give the country a truly great film called *42ⁿᵈ Street*.

Rian was embarrassed but Humph reached over and shook his hand firmly.

"Congratulations, sir."

"Thank you but no 'sir' nonsense. I'm still just a poorly paid newspaper hack trying to make a living anyway he can."

Humph couldn't help but smile. Unlike some of the murder suspects he'd interviewed of late, this now-nationally renowned Brooklynite didn't have an ounce of pretension about him. He'd be a Brooklyn luminary for the rest of his life, even if he ended up living it in Hollywood.

Humph rose to leave.

"Hold on, Humph. None of this script success means I don't have eyes and ears around Brooklyn. I grew up here."

Humph let himself drop back down in the chair with enough force to almost knock it on its side. He shot his right leg to the side just in time to stop it from tipping over.

"I happen to know—I won't say how—a made guy, a mob dandy. My aunt took him in when he was about 10. Apparently, the kid already knew some bad people. Anyway, he's at least 20 now and he drives a Packard 12. Nobody that age has ever owned a car like that."

"Mob, obviously," said Humph.

Rian nodded.

"He gave me a lift the other day. I needed to go to Beaver Street in Manhattan."

"Beaver Street. What the hell for?" Humph asked.

"Delmonico's. America's first great restaurant. I wanted to find out if their menu had changed due to the Depression."

Humph said he was not going to ask for the answer to that question. It was the boy he was interested in.

Rian was forthcoming.

"He said—just in passing, you know, just conversation—that a guy named Gagliardi was thinking about buying Delmonico's. I told him, 'Fat chance'. They'll never sell.

"The kid was silent for a while. Then he said that this Gagliardi guy wasn't going to be denied. He was dreaming big. He said this mob guy actually said at one point, 'Broadway or bust!'"

Rian said he didn't know if he meant Broadway literally or whether it was just a statement that meant New York or bust.

That was the second time Humph had encountered the Broadway or bust idea.

"I owe you one, Rian, no matter how you spell your name." With that he shook the newspaperman's hand.

Back on the street, Humph found a phone. He called Higgins.

"Gagliardi's our man without the slightest doubt. I'll explain later."

When he finally got back to Henry Street, he grabbed the late edition of several papers and hurried to his room. Moments later, there was a gentle knock at the door.

The bottle of Irish whiskey was already in his hand as he answered the door.

Eve and Rebecca greeted him.

Not seeing Duff, he felt momentarily agitated but after several seconds he recovered enough to kiss both girls on the cheek.

"We have a plan," said Eve.

Humph stared, frowning.

"What nonsense are you proposing?"

Rebecca stood and spent a moment pushing down her dress, which had risen while sitting. Humph couldn't help but follow her long fingers pressing on her thighs.

When the three were settled, Eve said the plan was simple and she and Rebecca were more than ready to pull it off.

"We're going to seduce this Gagliardi guy. From everything you've told us, and your talkative Irish investigator friend, he'll be easy pickings. The bigger the ego, the harder they fall."

"And then?" said Humph.

"And then we'll say we know his game and that we want part of the action."

Humph was dumbfounded.

"Eve, Eve... You're talking, you and Rebecca, of prostituting yourselves to solve a case."

Eve cocked her head and smiled at Humph.

"No damn way, Eve. Out of the question. That's the most horrid idea I've ever heard. No, no, no!"

Eve, her face still adorned with a cock-eyed smile, finally answered:

"We've already, Rebecca and I, invited Gagliardi to the night of his dreams. A friend of mine, from the stripper days we don't talk about anymore, has accepted a little bribe to give us use of the biggest bedroom in her bordello. She calls it the vice-presidential suite, a surprisingly honest acknowledgement of the fact that the room doesn't quite meet luxury standards."

Humph had no idea how to respond to his firebrand daughter, cheered on by the encroaching presence of a Latina-challenge glare from Rebecca.

Eve finally said:

"You look like a man who needs shut eye. Don't fight it. We're going to take care of things." With that, plus a smile from Rebecca, they disappeared.

After he heard them reach the bottom of the stairs and open the door to the building, Humph frowned, not so much in puzzlement, which was certainly his state, but also in a curmudgeonly sense. Was he getting too old and cynical to remain open to new ideas, fresh avenues of investigation, and particularly avenues offered by young women?

Not long afterwards, the whiskey got the best of him and he dozed off fully dressed. While he slept, a junior constable knocked on his door. His touch was tentative for he knew "the Humph's" reputation. He retreated and reported at the precinct that the detective wasn't home.

Also while he slept, Rebecca appeared at his door. She had no fear of disturbing the big detective. In fact, she knew he was more concerned about not disturbing her. However, her open-palm slaps on the door brought no response either.

No one could have guessed how Humph decided to spend what was already a disturbing night. After about an hour's sleep, he grabbed the table with two hands and hauled himself to his feet. He then staggered all the way to Duffy's. Sober, Humph would have been surprised by his actions. Better than anybody, he knew there was no tranquil twilight on offer at Duffy's.

By the time he got to Bowery, he was becoming alert. He was still vaguely annoyed about having let Eve and Rebecca put themselves in such danger.

Once inside Duffy's place and settled with a glass that he knew he shouldn't touch, he rapidly summarized the latest developments in the case, ending with the foolhardy intervention by the girls.

"That's no friggin' assault, Humphster. Sounds like a splendid strategy. Big guys like you and prickly bastards like me aren't always the best swords in the armory. Think about it. A guy who thinks he's Señor Suave and two females with a ton of female wiles... Bugger doesn't stand a chance."

"If he gets a whiff of what they're after, my girl, and dear Rebecca, are goners."

"You truly care for your dear Rebecca, I see."

"Go to hell, Duff!"

Humph walked around the room several times until Duffy said, "Put on the brakes. You're making me dizzy."

"Who knows," said Duffy. "They got a better chance of getting inside than you do."

Humph slid down the little sofa, his legs delineating south by southeast.

"I give up, Duff." He explained that his hands were tied until Higgins and his boys came up with something to connect the mob to Broadway. And now there was another impediment to his investigation, the girls confronting the main subject without the slightest evidence against him.

Duffy approached and sat in the skinny space left by Humph's sprawling legs.

"Lad, my biggest busts began with me accusing people who seemed to be pure as snow."

Humph sat up, giving Duffy some space.

"No offence, Duff, but it has often struck me that there are as many innocent buggers in jail as guilty ones because of your Irish charm before Irish judges."

"Be that as it may, my friend. I get the bad ones."

Humph couldn't argue with that.

Duffy stood and returned to his chair. Humph turned onto his left side. His feet remained on the floor but there was still room for his torso and head to fit on the sofa. He was snoring before Duffy opened a new bottle.

CHAPTER 23

IN the morning, Humph was relieved that he hadn't touched a drop of whiskey at Duffy's. He went home to await word from the girls and Higgins, in that order. If he didn't hear from Eve and Rebecca by noon, he would start a search. He would drag Duffy out of bed to help him.

Higgins got in touch first.

"You'd have to come down here for details but, while we didn't strike gold, we found some traces of gold dust here and there. People we believe to be part of the mob have their fingers in three pies that we know of. We've got Broadway workers who will testify that one or more of their elected union representatives have suddenly withdrawn from the contract talks, or a least the discussion by union members of what they want.

"They didn't mention seeing any violence or hearing any threats but the replacement union execs didn't seem to be seriously listening to the members' demands. Some said they thought they were being friendly towards the members but were nothing but smarmy instead."

Higgins said he had installed undercover cops as union members in all three cases. He added that there was other possible evidence of mob involvement but it was yet to be substantiated.

"Your case here is starting to stretch my manpower pretty thin, Humph. One thing you could do for me is go back and see your buddy, the president of the Broadway League. I'll tell you later what I want you to try to learn from him. I gotta go now."

He hung up before Humph could tell him about the scheme the girls cooked up the day before.

Humph phoned the Broadway League using the direct line its president had given him. He got an appointment for the following afternoon.

He then phoned Duffy.

"Rise and shine, old sod," he said without even a hello.

Humph then bathed his Duffy's curses for what must have been a full minute.

"Glad to see you're in top form, Duffy."

Before Duffy could launch into another tirade, Humph told him he was needed on two fronts.

"I still haven't heard from Eve or Rebecca. That's on the top of our list, Duff. The second job is to go back to the Broadway League and pick the president's mind about suspicious investment in Broadway shows."

Duffy asked Humph to give him an hour to get presentable. When Duffy arrived at Humph's place, Duffy suggested they take a taxi to Eve's. This time Humph didn't argue. He was more desperate about Eve's fate than he let on. Duffy knew that.

When they entered Eve's flat, there was a note on the dining table.

"Dad, don't worry. It turns out that Rebecca knows almost as much as I do about fending off gentlemen with antsy hands. Gagliardi will have no choice but to see us both at the same time. We're also going to insist that he buy us supper in a respectable restaurant. That's going to be safe at least. I'm going to spin him a line about wanting a bigger role on Broadway than what I have now, you know, dancing and singing."

"Smart," said Humph upon reading Eve's plan. "That's my girl. Think about it, Duff. If Gagliardi wants to win her over, he'll dangle a great Broadway future before her eyes, and probably Rebecca's as well. He'll have to admit to connections that would enable him to do that. Let's hope he'll be as boastful as he's been in the past, you know, when he tried to tell people at that dance hall in Harlem that he was a big deal in the entertainment business."

Duffy was nodding.

"Humph, you should hire that girl as a detective."

The brilliance of Eve's plan removed a lot of the worry from Humph's shoulders but it didn't tell him how the night turned out and where she was. He didn't know where Gagliardi lived either. And what about Rebecca. All he could do was go to Tompkins Square and see if she was home.

"Taxi," said Duffy. It wasn't a question.

When they arrived, her door was locked. Unlike Eve's place, Humph didn't have a key.

He and Duffy crossed the street and sat in the park.

Instead of talking about the case, Duffy said he was considering taking up the habit of chewing tobacco.

"I was reading about it in one of those big magazines, you know, the national ones. It wasn't *Life*, it wasn't the *Saturday Evening Post*. What the hell was it? Oh, yeah. I remember now. It was the *Police Gazette*. They said chewin' tobacco was centuries and centuries old. Has to be something to it, right?"

Humph stared at his friend hard.

"What if I sent a huge gob of spit between your two shoes right now. What would you say?"

"I wouldn't say a word. I'd smack you one in the gob."

"And right you'd be to do so. So what's the difference between that and spitting your tobacco juices all over the place?"

Duffy didn't have an answer.

Finally Humph said,

"And why are you talking about chewing tobacco when my daughter is missing?"

Duffy knew his friend was on boil.

"You're better off drinking, Duff. God knows you'd never spit out whiskey."

Once, after a similar bizarre conversation with Duffy, Humph admitted to Eve that he wished he knew how the Irish detective's mind worked.

"Not like yours and mine, for sure," he added.

It was a beautiful fall afternoon. Duffy was hungover. Humph was exhausted from worry.

Suddenly, Duffy rammed his shoulder into Humph's. No words came out of his mouth. He just pointed.

Across the street, there was elegant Rebecca, approaching her door.

Humph was the first to his feet. He leapt over a young shrub and reached the sidewalk, only to be blocked by a sudden swarm of automobiles passing by. He called out "Rebecca!" but the traffic must have drowned out his voice because she didn't turn in recognition of her name.

Duffy did his best interpretation of running and reached the other side of the street seconds after Humph.

Rebecca had already entered her place. Humph thumped on the door and called her name.

A two-minute eternity later, Rebecca opened the door.

"Humph, dear Humph, what brings you here," she said, smiling broadly.

"You're kidding," said a clearly exasperated Humph.

Rebecca stared into his eyes. It seemed like the longest time because the big man's heart was thumping to beat the band.

Then she hugged him and kissed him on the mouth.

"Well, I'll be…" said Duffy.

Rebecca ushered them in, giving Duffy a swat on the back of his head.

Once seated, Humph said, albeit gently:

"Talk."

Rebecca gracefully knelt on the floor in front of him and took his hands in hers.

"Your girl is fine, Humph. She's a champion. More balls than any man I know."

Maybe it was just a release of tension but Humph laughed loudly, grabbed her and hauled her onto the sofa next to him. He didn't let go."

"If you let me go for a moment, Humph, I'll tell you how Eve's scheme worked out."

Reluctantly, he did.

Rebecca tossed him a sidelong smile and faced Duffy.

"This Gagliardi guy is charming. He's also kind of good-looking. The problem, at least for me, is that he knows it. He went for the fine restaurant idea. Before we knew it, we were in this fancy dancy restaurant on 55ᵗʰ Street East called l'Aiglon. Gagliardi was even able to jabber-jabber with the maître d' and waiters in French."

"And my Eve?" said Humph.

Rebecca chuckled at the memory.

"She was having convulsions trying not to laugh. Gagliardi was curious about why but Eve had the presence of mind to say she wasn't used to so much champers."

Rebecca added that Gagliardi's response, a laughing one, was that Eve must build up her tolerance by having more. He continued to keep her glass filled.

"If only he knew our Eve."

Humph had to laugh at that. It was true. She could keep up with a soldier.

"What did you ladies learn?"

With a sparkle in her dark eyes, Rebecca said the man had great taste in food.

Rebecca took Humph's hand again and said that they learned that he thought he was the new king of Broadway.

"He said he was on the verge of producing the most spectacular Broadway productions ever seen. He said he had purchased books for shows New Yorkers and tourists would line up to see and he had arranged enough financing to ensure productions that were guaranteed to be absolutely spectacular. He said it all as casually as if he was saying the sun will rise tomorrow."

Rebecca said Gagliardi spent absurd amounts of time talking about the subtleties of the food they were being served.

"It was as if he was avoiding talking about why we had been invited."

Humph asked:

"Did the evening end that way?"

"No. Not at all."

Rebecca said Eve made things real by asking if Gagliardi could make her a Broadway star, as an actor, not just a singer and dancer.

"Gagliardi's reaction at first," said Rebecca, "was that Eve had interrupted an intellectual discussion with a personal concern. He's that pretentious."

Humph continued to hold Rebecca's hand as if she were a physical link to Eve. He stared down into her eyes.

"It took a while but he finally said, 'Of course I can.'"

"Did he explain how he could do that?"

"In a way," Rebecca said. "He said he will own these new shows 100 percent. He said he could dictate who starred."

Rebecca let go of Humph's hand and said that when she brought up the subject of union control over actors, their salaries and their rights, Gagliardi put on this ugly smile and said those are things he and he alone will decide. He then said, 'Eve will be a star on the Great White Way, and so will you if you want to be.'"

This information was invaluable.

Seeing that Rebecca was at ease with how the evening went was a huge relief.

"But where is my Eve?" Before asking the question, Humph had taken both her hands.

"When we left the restaurant, Eve went with Gagliardi. In the restroom, before going, she told me she had a plan."

CHAPTER 24

THAT was all Rebecca knew. Humph had no choice but to go home and wait. Wait for what? He didn't really know.

Before leaving Rebecca's, Duffy told him he'd go to the restaurant on Fifth Avenue and nose around.

"You never know," he said.

Just after noon, Detective Higgins called.

"Your girl, Eve, she just called. She said our guy Gagliardi is going crazy over her. She said he just took her to a luxe apartment on Fifth Avenue. He said it was hers if she would agree to be his, if you know what I mean."

"Thank God she's OK. How did she get away to call you?"

"Gagliardi left her alone while he went to Brooklyn on business, or so he said. I'm sure he's got someone watching the place to make sure Eve doesn't leave while he's gone."

"Do you have the address on Fifth Avenue? I feel like taking her out of there. It's too dangerous."

Higgins advised against the idea.

He said Eve had been showing herself to be more than resourceful.

"I'm getting more impressed by her lights every day."

"Lights?" asked Humph.

"Yeah. She's one quick-thinking young lady. And gutsy in ways you'd never think to look at her."

He added that yes, her situation was dangerous, stowed away in an apartment belonging to a gangster.

"But she has one advantage as an investigator over you and I, Humph. She's a good-looking young woman who's not exactly shy around men. He'll want to impress her. From what you've told me about him, Gagliardi will want to boast. Knowing she's in Broadway show, I'm hoping he'll want to prove he's a Broadway bigshot, or about to become one."

As much as he wanted to, Humph couldn't argue with the detective's logic. To rush in and steal back his daughter would make her a marked woman at the theater.

"Keep me posted, detective. Daily if you can."

"Count on it."

Several hours later, Humph was still trying to use Rebecca and Higgins's words to relax when Duffy appeared at the door.

He plunked himself down on the bed and declined Humph's offer of tea. Instead, he pulled a flask out of his suitcoat pocket.

"T'is only my second nip today."

"So?" Humph asked.

"Surprise. Surprise," said Duffy, pausing to take another nip.

As Duffy savored the whiskey, Humph insisted. "So? Talk, Duff."

Duffy was clearly enjoying drawing out the suspense.

"As a former copper, you will appreciate the progress of my inquiries at the restaurant. I progressed from doorman, to maître d', to waiter, to manager and..." He paused to take another sip.

"And, and, and!"

Humph was exasperated, much to Duffy's amusement.

"And," said Duffy, "the manager got so pissed off with me he ushered me into the boss's office. Not just the boss but the owner of the restaurant, l'Aiglon. I think it means "eagle" or one of those other pointy-beaked birds I hate so much. They're the real reason I live in New York."

"Duffy!" shouted Humph.

Duffy betrayed a smirk that Humph wanted to swat.

"The owner, who sees quickly that I'm an Irishman to be reckoned with, spurts out the fact that our beloved Walton Gagliardi approached him several months ago. His spiel was that he had an investment opportunity guaranteed seven ways to Sunday. In a Broadway show Gagliardi himself was shepherding to success."

"The owner said Gagliardi was convincing. He boasted about other entertainment biz accomplishments. Then the spell was broken when Gagliardi casually added that he had tentacles that reached the Fulton Street Market and other restaurant suppliers, such as bakeries. He said Gagliardi didn't elaborate beyond those intimations but the visit left this famous restaurateur with indigestion for the next week."

Humph was suddenly beaming.

Finally he said, "Duffy, all I can say is that the devil inside you has a funny bone." He then got up and crash-landed a full bottle of Irish whiskey in front of his friend. While Duffy opened it, Humph got on the phone to Higgins and related the new proof that Gagliardi was invading Broadway.

Higgins said that was the best news he'd had all day, then added that his guys pretending to be members of various Broadway unions were starting to send in reports.

"Not enough to lock anyone away but by their sheer number they add up to circumstantial proof."

After a pause, he added:

"Don't worry, Humph. As soon as your girl calls I'll let you know."

Duffy was so pleased with his day's work that he worked the bottle to death and ended up passing the night on the floor. As for Humph, he barely partook. The stakes were too high to confront them with a depleted mind. He didn't have Duffy's nature-defying ability to resurrect himself from the dead on a daily basis. Christ would have been envious.

The next morning, he left Duffy snoring on the floor and sought breakfast and a moment to read the papers. Finally, unable to spend another day waiting for news, he went uptown to l'Aiglon and asked to speak to the owner. It took some finagling but a $5 bill in a bus boy's palm finally got him through. The wait staff had not yet arrived.

Humph found the owner standing in a corner at the back of a spacious office. It was as if he was fearing a visit from someone unfriendly.

"Were you expecting a visit from a certain Mr. Gagliardi or one of his representatives? You seem shaken."

Before the owner of the restaurant had a chance to answer, Humph explained that as imposing physically as he might be, he was one of the good guys, a private detective and a former NYPD officer now working closely with the precinct's chief of detectives on a mob-related case.

"I request a moment or two of your, time, sir."

By the time the owner sat at his desk, a modicum of color had returned to his cheeks.

"Did you end up investing in Gagliardi's enterprise?"

The owner, suavely dressed and, Humph was certain,

ordinarily an impressive presence, was still having trouble breathing. Finally he admitted he had no choice but invest. Two nights after Gagliardi's visit, he said four imposing men took a table near the front of the restaurant.

"Imposing?" asked Humph.

"Yes, big and scary. They all ordered spaghetti. Such plebian dishes are not on our menu. If they had ordered hot dogs, the effect would have been as alarming."

He said they did not demand to speak with him but they told the maître d' to inform me of their presence.

"Message received, loud and clear. I called my broker the first thing the next morning."

"How much did you invest?" asked Humph.

"The total investment was $57,500. That's all I could dig up on such short notice."

The dollar figure and the withdrawal transaction as well as the broker's name were evidence of a connection. Humph walked out into the sunshine on Fifth Avenue energized. His new goal was to find other Gagliardi investment targets. However he didn't know where to start. He went home hoping to find Duffy still there and restored.

When he got there, Humph saw that Duffy was up and about but as to whether he was restored, no one could ever divine that.

"Duffy! Ready to work? I think we need to go back to the Broadway League."

"You 'think'?"

"I know."

Duffy demanded time to scrub his face and shave.

While waiting, Humph called the League and told the secretary that a meeting was urgent. She checked with her boss and returned to the phone.

"He'll see you but you'll have to get here in half an hour."

"Duff!" Humph all but shouted.

"Get your butt in gear. We have to fly."

"Taxi?" Duffy asked on the steps down to the sidewalk.

"What else. And you're paying."

"Always worth the expense," Duffy replied with a smile.

By the time they got to the Broadway League office, the president was halfway out the door.

"Mr. King," said Humph with evident urgency. "A couple of quick questions, or rather requests. Please. This is urgent."

"Shoot," said King, waving to his receptionist to join them. He signed "scribbling". She brought her stenographer's pad.

Quickly, Humph explained that he uncovered a wealthy businessman who recently had been pressured into investing in Gagliardi's Broadway interests.

"This can be great evidence of his attempts to overrun Broadway. But I need contacts for as many other possible victims as you can provide. Who are the people who traditionally invest in new shows, who are their brokers, anything you can provide?"

King turned his back on them and led his secretary across the room. For several minutes, with his hand securing her left arm, he whispered in her ear. With her free right hand, and holding her pad in her pinioned left, she took rapid notes. Suddenly, King released her arm and returned to the doorway where Humph and Duffy waited.

His manner abrupt, he faced Humph and said, "My secretary will get you what you need. Good luck." A moment later he disappeared into the elevator.

Each of them took a chair in front of the secretary's desk. She consulted files in a nearby cabinet and returned to her desk to make phone calls, many of them. The process took a good 20 minutes.

Finally she stood and announced she had a few scraps of information for them.

Duffy wanted to plant a kiss on her cheek as Humph thanked her. Humph's well-trained peripheral vision enabled him to step in front of Duffy before the ex-cop's lips could land.

As they returned to Seventh Avenue, they agreed it was too late in the day to pursue the names they'd just elicited from the Broadway League. Duffy heartily agreed, saying there was a lady he needed to see in the Bronx. It wasn't the first time he'd mentioned her. Humph wished him well but Duffy's face soured when Humph said he'd probably need him at his sharpest the following morning.

CHAPTER 25

DESPITE what he had just told Humph about going up to the Bronx to see a lady friend, Duffy took a swig from his flask and headed for the nearest phone both. The idea of shortening his Bronx date was outrageous to the point of almost being obscene. Being "sharp first thing in the morning" was not part of his bag of investigative tricks.

A second nip fueled his short walk to the New York Public Library on Fifth Avenue. There must be phones in the library, he reasoned. Once inside, he got change at the information desk. In the booth, he pulled out the list of Broadway investors he'd gotten from the Broadway League. The list included a few home numbers. Being in a booth shielded Duffy from prying eyes so he deposited his flask on the floor between his feet, freeing his hands to take notes.

He struck out on the first few calls, finding a couple of the money men not available at home or the office, and two others who swore they had never been approached by shady-looking unknowns in the investment world.

On his 11th call, his question was met with a long pause, long enough for Duffy to reach down for his flask. Before he could take a sip, the man at the other end spoke, almost too quietly to be understood. After Duffy explained who he was and that he had just come out of a meeting with Able King at the Broadway League, the man assumed a normal speaking voice. Had he suspected that someone on his party line, perhaps a mobster, was listening to his calls?

Duffy asked if he'd be more at ease if they met in person. The man immediately said no to any public meeting.

"Come to my home," he said decisively. He gave Duffy his address, on Bouck Avenue in the East Bronx, somewhere east of Boston Road. Duffy had never heard of it. After he hung up, he didn't need another sip of whiskey to know it was taxi time.

Because it was uncharted territory for Duffy, the ride seemed to take forever. Humph was going to get a doozy of a transportation expense claim. When he arrived at the address on Bouck Avenue, he got out in front a row of attractive, attached brick homes. He felt he had stepped into a world that had nothing whatsoever to do with the clamor of the city.

He was let into the house by a maid. Duffy preferred dealing with maids than butlers. Very few butlers had Irish accents. Most were Englishmen. As for the maid, she betrayed no discernable accent as she led him into the salon.

A squat though handsome man rose to introduce himself, Martin Merriweather. However there was nothing merry about his demeaner. Duffy's phone call had opened a can of paranoia and fear. Duffy now wanted to know how justified it was.

196

Merriweather spilled his guts almost before Duffy settled into his chair. If only the majority of crooks were that obliging.

"Long story short," the man said, "greed got the better of me. I'm kicking myself to this day. I'm a wealthy man, I have investment income even now with this damn Depression. But like an idiot, when a stranger finagled an appointment with me at the office, all I could see were dollar signs. He said he represented a private group of money men who had plans for not just one but two Broadway shows that had sure-fire success written all over them. He said he and the other investors wanted to invest in any show I might be planning in the near future. The condition was that their names remain secret. The secrecy was for tax reasons. In return, I had to let these men control the investment as the development of the show progressed."

Merriweather paused and swallowed deeply.

"As I told you, I saw dollar signs. The two shows I'm already invested in are costing more money than I ever planned on spending. Broadway shows are always like that. We live in precarious times, detective, financially speaking. These secret investors were too good to be true, but I failed to heed that truth."

It was Duffy's turn to pause. No financial wizard, he wanted to be clear about what might be evidence of mob involvement. To give him time to think he asked Merriweather whether he might see to pouring him a drink.

"It's been a long day, sir."

Merriweather obliged, pouring a glass for himself as well.

Duffy explained that the police were trying to piece together a case against these mob manipulators of Broadway finances. They needed the names of these interlopers, dates, letters, and so on.

"But most of all, they need the names of existing shows that seemingly have wavered from the straight and narrow path in expense requirements, union involvement or departures from Broadway League practices. Pretty well anything you can recall."

Merriweather nodded continuously at all of Duffy's requirements.

"And lastly, Mr. Merriweather, would you kindly check the list the Broadway League provided me with and tell me if anyone on it has behaved suspiciously in recent months."

It was late by the time Duffy boarded a cab, too late to regale himself with a raunchy evening in the South Bronx. Disappointed in himself for cow-towing to Humph's request, he told the cabbie they were Bowery-bound.

When he got home, he phoned Humph. He didn't care if he woke him up. Getting him out of bed would be the equivalent of Humph getting him out of bed early the next day. Anyway, he was excited by his discoveries in the Bronx.

So was Humph, so much so that he absolved Duffy of the necessity to appear early the next morning. Humph hadn't heard a peep from Det. Higgins all day, which left him too on edge to sleep. Humph asked Duffy to join him so he could make full notes of Duffy's new evidence.

"Do I have to bring my own whiskey?"

Humph checked and came back on the line.

"Yes."

Before Duffy arrived, Humph phoned Rebecca. As the phone rang, he crossed the fingers of his left hand.

She had been asleep.

"If I'd heard anything about Eve you would have been the first to know. You know that."

There was a touch of admonishment in her voice but no more. Humph apologized. He knew that. He wished her good night.

When Duffy walked through the door, Humph was sitting at the table, littered with notebooks and pencils. To his left, positioned in front of the far end of the table, were two glasses.

Duffy decided to not immediately present Humph with the taxi receipts. Instead he offered his bottle. Humph poured drinks for them both. He was thirsty, a thirst brought on by the intensity of the evening's investigation in the northeastern Bronx and the lack of sexual release occasioned by the premature return downtown.

For almost three hours, Duffy talked and quaffed. Humph stopped him scores of times to demand clarification. Repeat a time sequence, or provide a precise name, suspicions vague and otherwise. Fortunately, Duffy had a bizarre capability of recalling tiny details even while being besotted by ordinary standards. Humph wondered often whether Duffy possessed something called eidetic memory, an insane ability to recall details, photographic or textual.

He once asked Duffy if he actually did have that extremely rare ability.

"I've never even heard that idiotic word. Must have been invented by a constipated Brit."

However the truth was, as Humph's eclectic reading proved, that the discovery of that kind of memory dated back to 1924, only nine years earlier. Even if he had it, Duffy would of course deny it. In his mind, he was everyman. He didn't even mind being dismissed as a bogger.

"We're all the same," he would say, "bogger or bullshitter."

Just before the sun rose, Humph stood, wandered to the end of the table and sat Duffy up straight. He sat next to him, his big hand holding the detective almost upright.

"You did well, my friend. Very, very well. I think we've got a case. Do you hear me?"

"Joy of joys," replied Duffy, eyes closed.

Humph had no idea whether Duffy was replying to his words or some fantasy in an obliterated mind.

The end of the table being no more than a foot from his bed, he half picked up and half shoved his friend onto the mattress. As for himself, he decided to go out and find an all-night diner with enough coffee to keep him awake until Det. Higgins would arrive at the precinct.

CHAPTER 26

AT 8:35 the next morning, Humph dumped nearly 20 pages of notes on the desk of Det. Higgins. Higgins then looked him in the eye and said, "Explain."

His eyelids drooping despite the coffee injection, Humph did his best. Finally, Higgins said he got the picture.

"Relax." It was almost an order. Higgins called in another detective and asked, "How fast can you read? I need the nuts and bolts of all this in 20 minutes." The young detective hurried away with the pile of notes.

Higgins and Humph were silent for several minutes. Finally, Humph muttered the word "Eve".

Higgins got up and lightly slapped Humph's cheeks to wake him up.

He started to return to consciousness. Minutes later, fresh coffee arrived.

Higgins didn't hurry him. He was awaiting the young detective's summary of Humph's notes.

Humph dozed off again without touching the coffee.

In Higgins's eyes, that was just fine. No matter what the young detective concluded from Humph's notes, Higgins knew he'd need time to do some deep thinking. He needed to separate the circumstantial from the solid evidence.

Humph was showing signs of reviving around 11 a.m. Higgins had already assigned five detectives—his entire stable—to explore the leads Humph had produced.

Most importantly, in the hours Humph slept, Higgins had received word that Eve and Gagliardi had been seen together at the entrance to the theater where Eve's show was rehearsing.

Two officers were ordered to shadow every movement by the two.

When Higgins relayed the news to Humph, he woke up as if he'd been doused with a gallon of ice water.

"Arrest the slimy bastard!" Humph said.

"We can't. Not yet," said Higgins, holding Humph's right forearm.

Humph continued to be agitated. It was the behavior of a man who'd been drinking heavily but he didn't smell like it. At the request of the detective, a burly constable came upstairs to the detective's floor.

"This man," said Higgins, "is a former cop and a friend of the department. He's panicking about the fate of his daughter who, at present, is in the hands of a man we want to put behind bars for life."

The constable had never been confided in like that. Instinct told him that this was a life-or-death situation.

As gently as a big man can move, he embraced Humph and led him to a holding cell downstairs. He didn't lock the door. Instead, he sat on a chair just outside it. He had been given written instructions on what to do if Humph challenged him:

"Bring him to me." It was signed: "Higgins."

The day dragged on. Higgins wanted news for himself as well as Humph. This was a big case for the department. In the past, he'd never before gotten permission to assign that many detectives to an investigation. Having that many men in the field but not getting any word from them made the wait even more exasperating.

Suddenly a shout from the stairwell and the sound of a body banging against the wall suspended his irritation. Curiosity took over.

A voice cried out, "Sir!". Then another shouted, "Higgins!"

Appearing first at the top of the stairs was the barrel-chested constable he'd assigned to monitor Humph, then, a split second behind, was the private eye.

The constable was almost out of breath.

"Sir, I tried to bring him to you as you requested but when he woke up he charged into me like I was there to hold him prisoner. Mr. Humph knocked me into the wall and barreled by me and up the stairs. I grabbed his shift and got him off balance enough to get by him on the stairs. Then he grabbed my uniform jacket and tried to pull past me. He was acting crazy, sir. I just wanted to get myself between you and him, sir."

Higgins thanked the constable.

"Under the circumstances, you did a fine job, young man. You're excused."

Before the constable reached the stairs, Humph hurried over to him.

"Sorry. I was in the middle of a bad dream."

Humph started talking to Higgins before they reached the detective's desk.

"I don't know whether I mentioned this to you before. I probably did but that was before Eve volunteered herself as a mob slave."

Higgins didn't interrupt. When Humph apologized to the constable it showed that he was back to his normal self.

Humph reminded Higgins that Prohibition was ending in a couple of months. This was October, he said, pointing at the calendar behind Higgins's desk.

"The nonsense ends in December. The speaks will die or at least convert to legal bars. We won't need to drink out of teacups, right."

Higgins nodded.

"What I now remember us talking about this summer, when we first started looking into the idea of the mob taking over Broadway. Their reason for doing so could be as simple as one, two, three. With booze legal again, the mob is going to lose millions and millions of greenbacks a year."

Higgins remembered the conversation.

"You asked me if I thought the mob would let that happen," said Higgins. "We agreed that their attempt to make Atlantic City's casinos theirs made perfect sense from that perspective, their urgent need to find another cash bonanza."

Humph nodded.

"And they were so desperate they even toyed with the idea of out-and-out war with the man who owned Jersey, Nucky Johnson. Nuck owned New Jersey."

"Then being the brilliant thinkers we are," said Higgins, "we concluded that the path of least resistance for the New York mob would be to swallow up the millions of dollars being thrown around by Broadway investors. They wouldn't have to fight another criminal enterprise."

"And on top of that," Humph said, "they could continue to expand Broadway across the river and give Nucky a share of proceeds from the greatest theater in the world, earned right there in New Jersey."

Higgins looked at Humph.

Humph smiled and nodded.

"Goodbye Prohibition," said Humph.

"And hello Broadway," added Higgins.

The back and forth of two people who thought the same way greatly reduced Humph's distress. After a pause, he said:

"This brings me to the thought that set off fireworks in my head as I slept," said Humph. "Who was in charge of the mob's Prohibition business? He would have had to be one of the top made men. Do you think he could be the boss behind Gagliardi's Broadway schemes, the man Gagliardi answers to?"

Higgins nodded in the affirmative.

"Makes absolute sense, Humph."

"So, my friend," said Humph, "are we tracking him the way we're tracking Gagliardi and his boys?"

"You mean, his 'boys and girls,'" added Higgins, renewing his stare at Humph.

"Yes!" As Humph said it, he leaned forward and slammed the detective's desk. My dream down in that holding cell was that I knew what was going on but no one else did. No one was bird-dogging this mob biggie. No one was asking if he knew of Eve. I shouldn't have underestimated you, Higgins. Sorry. Seriously. Even in my nightmares I shouldn't have come after you. You would have remembered the connection on your own."

Higgins told Humph he was no use to anyone at the moment. He should go home and sleep, not drink.

"Even if Duffy bangs on your door, don't answer."

Humph said that "No truer words had ever been spoken on the Lower East Side."

That night, around midnight, the phone rang. Following Higgins's advice, Humph didn't answer. A few hours later, around 3:30 a.m., a constable knocked on his door. He didn't say hello. Instead he handed Humph a piece of paper and waited at the door.

"Tried to reach you last night. No reply. We nailed a union buster. Hoping interrogation will widen our net.

Drop by any time. H."

Humph stood again and nodded to the copper at the door. The constable didn't nod back. He just left. He'd fulfilled his assignment without uttering a word.

The next morning, Humph skipped his usual coffee and ignored the headlines at the newsstand.

When he arrived at the precinct, he learned that Higgins had yet to appear.

"However, there's a message for you, sir."

Humph wasn't used to the "sir" treatment. But he was growing tired of the standard response to his "No sir allowed, sunny. Name is Humph. Nothing else."

Invariably, the response was, "Yes, sir."

Humph poured himself a coffee that by its smell had been servicing the night shift. He didn't touch it until he went upstairs and sat in front of Higgins's desk.

Higgins arrived 40 minutes later.

"Got your message," Humph said by way of hello.

Higgins's face, usually unexpressive, was strangely severe.

"That girl you like, that make-up girl at Eve's show…" He didn't finish the sentence.

"Yeah," Humph replied with smile. "Never mind her. What about this mob guy you corralled last night?"

"On the surface, it makes no sense but they're one in the same," said the detective. "Rebecca is the brains behind the Broadway infiltration."

"Fuck that," yelled Humph.

Higgins stood up and called out a name. "Detective Mulroney!"

CHAPTER 27

HUMPH had been turned to stone as if hit by a right cross from Max Baer. Max 2 had become Max 1, world heavyweight champion, by defeating Max Schmelling. Humph ceased all movement, all thought and almost all breathing.

Det. Mulroney arrived a minute later. He had a kind face. When he looked at Humph, his eyes said he felt his pain as much as did.

Higgins bent down and took Humph's hand. He said he was sorry but he had to follow the evidence.

Humph looked at him blankly. Then he let go of Higgins's hand and stood. Without looking back, he walked down the stairs to the first floor, keeping his left hand on the wall for balance.

Upstairs the detectives looked at each other. Not a word

was spoken.

That evening, at the precinct bar that might soon be history when Prohibition ended, Humph was spotted. Duffy sat at the bar with him. The bar had grown almost silent, a rarity. Humph and Duffy were near to blows but they were largely regarded as eccentrics, especially Duffy, and no one really knew how to intervene.

Det. Mulroney edged closer. Humph's head was facing away from Duffy's face. Mulroney tried to imagine the power a body like Humph's could summon. The Irishman wouldn't stand much of a chance. If he'd seen that in any other bar he'd bail. But he couldn't escape the notion that Humph was facing away from his longtime friend for one reason. He didn't want the Irishman igniting his fuse.

Mulroney steeled himself and settled on Humph's right, away from Duffy.

Softly he said, "A few words. I can tell you why we concluded what we did. But the last thing I want is to make this a bar room discussion or bar room brawl. Can we find a table?"

After the two pushed through what appeared to be half the entire police force, they found a corner table. Neither ordered a drink.

Mulroney said, "Prefer to find a park bench outside?"

Humph nodded.

They started walking in silence towards Henry Street. Humph was leading the way. A block before his place, in front of the newsstand he visited every morning, Humph turned around and said to the detective:

"I appreciate your discretion. You can say what you need to say to me at my place. I just want to tell you that I'll need a ton of convincing. This accusation against Rebecca is insane. She has been an enormous help in my investigation. It simply doesn't figure."

The detective nodded.

"I don't deny that you might be right, Humph. I just

want to talk."

Humph wondered whether Mulroney, despite the Irish name, was some new kind of detective, considerate, smart, a good listener. In fact, those were all the qualities he felt he had, not that he would ever boast about them.

Once inside Humph's place, he offered the detective a drink.

"Maybe later" was the reply.

In Humph's eyes, he just climbed another notch as a professional.

Humph, however, reached for a bottle, explaining that he was the victim at the moment.

Mulroney smiled. After all, imbibing victims, like criminals, were more talkative.

It was Humph who put reality on the table.

"What was it that made you finger Rebecca as the mob's infiltrator, their go-between with the unions?"

"She went to bed with Gagliardi."

Humph stared at the detective in disbelief. Finally he spoke.

"So what?"

It took a while for him to simmer down. He didn't want to admit it but he was shocked. Immediately, the absurdly logical part of him tried to figure out why he was shocked. He had never romanced her. They had kissed but the kisses were exchanges of sweetness, nothing else. Had he wished they were more than that. He couldn't answer himself right away. But by God he did like her, her company, her mind, her looks.

Was he, in her eyes, just a nice guy who in the end was just an ordinary guy? That made some kind of sense to him because she was unusually beautiful. He knew he was not in her league.

And, he had to admit, Gagliardi was handsome as hell.

"Go on," he said to Mulroney.

Mulroney answered that, in itself, sleeping with the main suspect in a case was not a crime.

"However, over the course of the next few days, we spotted her visiting two union reps from different Broadway unions."

Humph interrupted.

"I repeat, so what? She could have gotten to know them in any number of ways. She's been working on shows for a lot of years."

"But," said the detective, "she invited each of the men to Gagliardi's swank Fifth Ave apartment. We don't know what they talked about exactly but clearly it was something Gagliardi told Rebecca to arrange."

"This isn't making the slightest sense," Humph said, this time with an edge to his voice. "It sounds like two coincidences piled on top of each other."

"I disagree, Humph." He said using Rebecca, a well-known face backstage in many a theater made so much sense we could forget the appearance of coincidence. They would have agreed to go to Gagliardi's with Rebecca because she was known and trusted. Nothing bad would happen to them at Gagliardi's apartment.

Begrudgingly, Humph nodded his head. There was logic in what he said.

"If Gagliardi was about to put down big money to mount a new show, perhaps he wanted to get the lay of the land and find out if some money in the right pockets could reduce union demands when the time came. How long has Rebecca been catching fish for Gagliardi?"

He and Humph stared at each other in silence for a moment. Finally the detective said, "Now you see why we have to investigate Rebecca. Humph couldn't deny the reasoning.

While Humph was pouring a drink, the detective told him they know Rebecca has never been in trouble with the law, except perhaps for the time she came down to the cop shop to complain about the heavy-handed way our constables rousted the squatters at Tompkin's Square.

Humph sat across from the detective.

"I was a witness to it," he said. "Nobody in blue seemed to give a damn that these people were starving and homeless."

Mulroney said he personally agreed with Humph, and by extension, with Rebecca.

"But let me remind you that a socially unpopular decision like that one isn't usually made by cops. Sniff around and you'll smell city hall, people in suits wanting to make money out of misery one way or another."

Once again, Humph couldn't argue with the detective.

He then drained his glass and poured another. This time, the detective reached toward him with a glass in his hand.

"I poured another shot because I'm trying to figure out how to pursue my next concern. Where is my Eve in all this. My understanding was that Gagliardi invited her to move into his place to be his main squeeze. Eve was delighted because she would be in a good position to get first-hand knowledge of any attempts to corrupt or compromise the unions. She deserves a medal for that.

"However, you have a million detectives blanketing Broadway at the moment and I've had no news whatsoever about Eve. And if she was supposed to be Gagliardi's girl, how did it come about that he bedded Rebecca. He has laid claim to the only two women I deeply care about. Is that a coincidence as well?"

Mulroney could see the pain in Humph's eyes.

"May I use your phone?"

Humph just pointed to it.

CHAPTER 28

DET. Mulroney phoned Humph the next morning.

"I could come to your place or you could come here and talk to me, Det. Higgins and a couple of the boys who've been investigating. There's no earth-shaking news to tell you but you're a man who clearly appreciates the bits and pieces that make up an investigation. You're an important part of it. That goes without saying."

Humph appreciated the call. On his way to the precinct he ignored the morning papers. The detective branch would know anything the papers did. He corrected himself. That was usually true but surprisingly often the papers got information the cops didn't.

Higgins raised his hand to greet him when he got to the second floor. Humph took his usual seat in front of his desk.

WAYNE CLARK | Busted on Broadway

Mulroney and the others are on their way. Higgins said, "Mulroney wanted to talk to them away from here, in a diner. Not sure why."

Humph said he spent hours with Mulroney yesterday.

"A good man. He impressed me more than a little."

Higgins smiled.

"I guess we have the same taste in detectives."

Suddenly they heard a shouting match in the stairwell.

"No fucking way. She's a whore and not to be trusted."

"Shut up, you idiot." Both Higgins and Humph realized that was Mulroney's voice.

At the top of the stairs, Mulroney and the four men behind him, presumably detectives, saw that they were the object of everyone's attention, including their boss, Det. Higgins.

"Det. Mulroney. Could you possibly summarize this dawn dispute?"

Mulroney apologized then nodded toward Humph.

"Det. Morris feels that Eve is our suspect, not Rebecca."

Humph was halfway out of his chair, a vein pulsing on his left temple, when Higgins ordered Det. Morris to explain first of all why he felt it was necessary to raise his voice to Det. Mulroney. He didn't get a straight answer. Instead, an argument erupted among the detectives. It lasted a good 15 minutes, some of the detectives clinging to theories that women were untrustworthy or opportunistic by nature. They cited examples from previous cases they'd worked on.

Higgins slapped his palm on the desk, finally producing silence.

"So much for my crack team of detectives. Anyone eavesdropping would suspect you were a gaggle of crotchety, gossipy women. And here you are leaping to denigrate two respected and talented women who volunteer their services to the NYPD. At least," Higgins said, "they have earned their money."

A voice from the back asked: "By the way, how much have we paid them?"

Det. Mulroney laughed.

Then Higgins said, "I'm laughing too. None of you dolts has come up with anything real in this case, at least not compared to these ladies. For some reason, you seem to want them to be guilty. What Det. Mulroney and I find funny is that they're not getting paid a cent. You guys, who cost me a lot of money, have produced nothing."

Humph's heartbeat had returned to normal upon hearing the senior detective's masterful put-down.

He couldn't bear for Eve's motives to be questioned as if she were a tramp. She was as principled and brave as any of them. This was another time when he was thankful for having left the force.

Higgins asked if any of them had personally witnessed Rebecca with Gagliardi or Broadway union members.

That produced some positive replies. One said he saw her being let into Gagliardi's apartment on a night when Eve was absent. "Ditto the next night. And they didn't leave the place the next day."

Higgins interrupted, asking almost rhetorically, "And that was the basis for a conclusion that Eve had been ousted and Rebecca was now Gagliardi's leading lady?" The detective didn't dare defend his conclusion.

Another detective, apparently assigned to trail Eve, had noticed her absence from Fifth Avenue.

Trying to stay a step ahead of Det. Higgins, he stated that he definitely didn't come to any immediate conclusions about her.

"In fact, I lost her for about three hours that evening. I finally found her at her theater rehearsing a dance number. Not being a real fan of that kind of dance, I hid out backstage, holding a bunch of flowers to give me cover."

Det. Mulroney interrupted. "If anything detective, that bouquet made you more conspicuous. No one brings flowers for rehearsals. Continue."

"She went home that night but the next morning she went straight to the head office of the Broadway League on Seventh. I must say that girl's energy was running me ragged. Anyway, by sweet-talking the office secretary, I learned that this dancer, of all people, had been admitted to the office of the League's chief financial officer. Why? I never figured that out. She spent three hours in his office. It was from that, and Eve's close association with Gagliardi, that I concluded she was trying to use some mob blackmail tactic on him. Why else would such a respectable man have the time of day for a girl like Eve."

The throbbing was returning to Humph's temple.

To complete the session, Higgins asked the remaining detectives one by one if they had anything to report. Several did but they were mostly inconclusive observations. One mentioned seeing low-level union officers at a regular monthly meeting. They introduced a union member who wanted to volunteer his services to the union executive. The new guy talked of run-of-the-mill complaints and contract violations he'd observed. He also yammered on about larger issues sure to come up in the next contract talks. If this guy was mob, no one could have guessed it. Nothing was threatening. Everything sounded reasonable. Everything he said was just advice. On top of that, he talked just like one of the boys."

Higgins stood up, his frown growing by the minute.

"At last, some real insight into what is really happening. OK boys, get out of here."

After everyone had descended the stairs, far more quietly than they'd ascended an hour earlier, Humph turned to Higgins and said, "Is this what you deal with every day?"

Higgins didn't reply. But his silence did.

Higgins and Humph stepped out a while later. Neither

dictated where they were going but both walked around a corner to a featureless diner called Copless. What that meant, neither had any idea. The menu contained no anti-cop entries. The world was changing since the start of the Depression. Citizens were quietly rebelling. Quietly because they had no resources, no standing. All they had was numbers, people willing to push back. The police never knew the enemy they so casually beat down. They didn't know they weren't enemies. They were just down-on-their-luck Americans who were starving through no fault of their own. But orders were orders.

Perhaps the name of the diner was a simple, subtle statement the down-and-out of the neighborhood understood. The name was code for feelings they shared. Whatever it meant, Humph and Higgins were served with a smile. Then they remembered they were out of uniform.

Over apple pie, they tried to distill actual evidence from the morning's nonsense. By the time both rose, leaving a nickel tip on the table, they agreed the meeting had been damn near a waste of time.

"Only one thing we can do now," said Humph. Higgins, brushing some pie crust crumbs from his vest, looked up and said, "Duffy?"

Humph nodded. In silence they returned to the precinct where Higgins made enquiries about the Irishman's whereabouts.

Because Duffy had been working undercover, no one really knew where he was or where he had been the night before.

"When in doubt," Humph said, "especially before noon, the odds are that he's at home sleeping one off."

When they got to the Bowery tenement, they were surprised their knock didn't elicit cursing. Duffy was up and dressed. In an almost mannerly way, he led them to his sitting room. Humph's antennae were on full alert. A moment later, he and Higgins stood stock still. Feet away, in the room's only easy chair, was none other than Rebecca, the woman thought to be a mob go-between by more than one detective only hours before.

Duffy stepped in front of them and bowed deeply with a sweeping motion of his arm that indicated the person in the easy chair.

"May I present…"

"Shove it, Duff," Humph shouted. "What is going on?"

Duffy enjoyed his own touch of theatrics so much he didn't resent Humph's raised voice in the slightest.

With a flash of the most beautiful teeth on the Lower East Side, Rebecca said to Duffy: "May I?"

Duffy chuckled and nodded.

Before she could say a word, Humph uncharacteristically blurted out:

"Did you bed Gagliardi?"

"No!" replied Rebecca. *Me da asco.*"

"Humph, ask for a translation," said Duffy, smirking.

"It means 'He disgusts me!" Rebecca held Humph's eyes making him think his accusation now made her find him disgusting.

Higgins came to Humph's defense.

"Humph never thought that but several detectives believed you did at a meeting this morning believed you were sleeping with him. Their only evidence was astonishing. They said he was dark and handsome. You were dark and stunning. Therefore…"

"Cretins!" Rebecca was halfway out of her chair before she responded to Higgins's hands motioning her down.

"That's what men are, catatonic cretins!" Her dark eyes now looked black.

When she calmed down, Higgins asked her first of all to explain why Eve, his supposed bedmate, had left and she appeared to move in to replace her.

As Rebecca waited for her fury to abate, she looked at

Duffy and motioned for him to pour a drink.

Everyone waited for her to sip it.

"Because…" Her voice rang out loudly. She paused as if realizing that her pent-up anger had turned the volume knob to the right. "Because Eve told me Gagliardi had decided that Eve's feminine wiles and her intimate knowledge of the theater would make her irresistible to older union officers. She was his best ticket backstage. He didn't want her wasting her talents hanging around his apartment."

Higgins asked if that was the last time she saw Eve at Gagliardi's apartment.

"No. She came back the next day for clothes. Gagliardi had already gone out."

Humph couldn't hold back any longer.

"What did she say? How was she? Tell me everything, Rebecca."

Rebecca stood and approached Humph. She took his hand and led him to the sofa, forcing Duffy to move to the easy chair. She motioned to Higgins that there was room for him to stay at the end of the sofa. She sat Humph down at the other end, still holding his hand. She had seen the fatherly concern in his eyes when he asked her about Eve. There was nothing cretin-like about Humph.

"Here's what I know," said Rebecca.

"Eve said she pretended to be infatuated with Gagliardi the instant she moved in. She said his chest protruded so much with primitive male pride that he had no choice but become magnanimous a moment later when she apologized that this was her time of the month. He gave her his bed and he slept on a visitor's bed in another room. She made a point of getting out the door the first thing the next morning."

"And?" said Higgins.

"She made a B-line for the office of the president of Actors' Equity Association, the biggest of all Broadway unions. She said she had to almost plead to get in to see him. You never know when an actor's skill will come in handy. She convinced the secretary that the president's life was in grave danger. She said a mob plot to assassinate him had been discovered."

"Not far from the truth," said Higgins, fascinated.

"Eve told me that once inside this guy's office, she hiked up her skirt a bit and marched purposefully to the chair before his desk. She said she knew she had his attention. He was middle-aged but not unattractive. He probably still had an eye for the opposite sex."

After admitting to the union president that there had been no direct threat on his life, Eve told him there was something just as unthinkable going on. Police had learned of a direct threat to the future of Broadway.

Duffy had been quietly sipping away while Rebecca recounted what he already knew.

Humph noticed that Duffy's Irish lilt was more pronounced as he told Higgins and Humph that after Eve left the apartment and Rebecca seemingly replaced her, he followed Gagliardi to Brooklyn, to a non-descript hole in the wall labelled Bensonhurst Men's Club.

"I know the place," Duffy said. "If that's a men's club, I'm English."

He said it was really the headquarters for Salvatore Maranzano, better known as mob boss Little Caesar. He was the de facto mayor of Bensonhurst.

"Not being Sicilian, I've never managed to enter the club. I doubt if they'd even allow me to deliver a pizza."

Everyone sat silent waiting for a conclusion.

Duffy played the room like a grand entertainer. However, he sensed that Humph was close to landing a very big fist on his coffee table.

"When Gagliardi exited, he was with Maranzano. They were surrounded by overweight guys whose arms found no room to rest straight down at their sides. They were like 300-pound birdlings, or whatever you call chicks, preparing to attempt flight. The key thing I took from this is that at the center of this wrestling ring, he shook hands with Maranzano, who clapped him on the back to boot. They had not met for a game of dominoes."

Higgins said that was the sort of information he was after.

"But that's not all, Mr. Chief of Ds."

Duffy played the pause to the fullest.

"Duff! Stop playing games."

"It'll cost you, Humph."

Humph slapped himself on the forehead, turned to Duffy and said "Name it, you son of a..."

"No need to finish your blasphemous sentence, my friend.

"I followed Maranzano's lump of muscle to guess where?"

"No more guessing games, Duffy." It was Higgins speaking.

"Well, sir, truth be told, this lump of muscle went straight to the union office, the United something or other. The very one where dear Eve met with the union biggie.

"Were you sober enough to make notes of all this," Higgins asked without the slightest embarrassment?"

Duffy smiled, raised his glass and stared at his old boss.

"I've been taking notes since half your boys were born. Of course I did. You're almost sitting on them. If you take your eyes off Rebecca and asked her to stand, you'll see she's been sitting on them, keeping them nice and warm just for you."

Rebecca stood and there the notes were, under the sofa cushion.

"You're one crazy Irishman," said Higgins. "Wish I had more like you."

"Thanks for the compliment, sir."

Duffy then faced Rebecca.

"Now, my dear, what say you to a fun little soirée?"

Rebecca laughed, stood, embraced Duffy and said:

"My dear defender, thank you for all you've done but in case you hadn't noticed, I am spoken for." With that she took Humph's hand, dragged him to his feet and said, "Gentlemen, I'm not sure where you will find me next, but I'm sure your detecting skills won't fail you. Good day all."

As he and Rebecca walked down to the street, Humph realized he'd never been more speechless. What the hell was it about women?

CHAPTER 29

REBECCA took Humph back to her place on Tompkins Square. She couldn't explain why she didn't want to go to his place. She guessed that he'd always be a detective there. She was exhausted with investigations, accusations and a total disregard for good human beings, Eve being the main one, herself perhaps being the second. She was a damn make-up artist, a real artist in the most creative world on earth, Broadway. I want you all, coppers and mobsters, to leave me alone!"

Humph caressed her cheek.

"And I love you," she said.

Only one woman had ever said that to him. Eve's mother.

Humph felt paralyzed. Long ago, he'd told himself he could never replace Eve's mom. That was the one love that was meant to be. He'd told himself that so many times that the most beautiful woman in the world could pass him by with a smile and he would feel nothing but emptiness.

Rebecca was different. He didn't know why and he didn't know how to respond.

Rebecca had no whiskey in the cupboard but she had wine, red and white, a bottle of the latter already chilling in the ice box. Although the outside temperature was already dropping as fall took hold, Humph's temperature had risen with her confessed love for him. He was worried out of his mind by Eve and at the same time floating happily in Rebecca's presence.

"I'll take a glass of white," Humph said. "I'm overheating."

An hour later he suggested Rebecca put another bottle of white to chill.

Her back was to him as she wound up the Victrola. She faced him again as the strains of Duke Ellington's *Sophisticated Lady* began to fill the room.

She extended her arm inviting Humph to dance. He got to his feet but like a damn man he chose to ask questions about the Victrola.

"You don't see many of those anymore. Didn't the company go bankrupt not many years back?"

Before answering, she gently but insistently pulled him to her, taking the initiative to actually wrap his right arm around her waist.

"That's how I could afford it. They were selling off all their inventory and insane prices. I paid $25. Ten years before it could have cost me hundreds and hundreds. Now shut up."

When the song ended, Rebecca cranked up the old machine again. This time, Humph didn't hesitate to hold her close. She didn't notice that their swirls led them smoothly to a spot in front of the ice box.

"Do you think the next bottle of white has chilled?" Humph asked.

"Watch out, mister, or I'll chill."

"An idle question. That's all."

Before retrieving the bottle, Rebecca gave him a little hug.

Minutes after they settled on the sofa with their glasses, the phone rang. Rebecca growled as she rose to answer it.

"Eve!" Rebecca exclaimed.

Humph could hear Eve's voice at the end of the line. She was speaking urgently.

"Of course. Of course. I'll be waiting for you," said Rebecca. She had a huge smile as she turned back to Humph. Like Humph, she'd been worried by Eve's three-day-long absence.

She explained that Eve was fine, just excited. She had come up with real evidence linking the mob and Broadway's biggest union.

"Thank God she's OK." Humph threw his arms around Rebecca, lifting her briefly off the ground and spinning her around. Putting her down, he suddenly became business-like.

"May I use your phone? I've got to reach Det. Higgins."

He didn't have a home number for the detective, forcing him to call the precinct and badger someone into reaching Higgins and telling him to urgently call him at Rebecca's number.

"I hope you don't mind me inviting him. I know it was only a couple of hours ago that you said you want cops to leave you alone."

For a moment, Humph thought she was glaring at him, then she said coyly, "I've been known to change my mind."

While waiting for Eve and Higgins, Rebecca made coffee.

"Why did you want Higgins here tonight?"

"Because he can put things in perspective in terms of what we have and what we need still before making any kind of arrest. And we don't know whether Eve has been able to communicate with him since resurfacing just now."

Then he added, "…and he knows the history of the mob in New York."

Higgins arrived before Eve.

"We meet again," he said to Rebecca with a Gaelic twinkle in his eye and gratefully accepted the cup of coffee she handed him. "It's been a very, very long day."

Humph asked if he'd spoken to Eve that evening. He said he'd been in the dark like everybody.

"I pray she has some useful information. My boys finally started bringing in a few little tidbits after the browbeating I gave some of them."

It was half an hour before Eve arrived. She apologized for the delay.

"I absolutely had to find a friend at the theater to give me a bottle of whiskey. I need to unwind."

"Know that feeling, Eve," said Rebecca approaching her. Eve extended the bottle to her but Rebecca pushed it away and embraced Eve.

Right behind Rebecca was Humph. He took the bottle in his left arm but still he had enough reach to hug both women with his right.

For the next five minutes, Humph held the floor, peppering Eve with questions. "Did anyone hurt you? Have you eaten? Have you slept? Did you have to escape? Was there any violence? Did you have to do anything against your will?" The latter was the only question that devoured Humph at the moment.

"No, Dad. No, no, no. I swear!"

Eve said she'd tried to reach him by phone but there was no answer.

"I see why," she said with a smile, pointing her glass towards Rebecca.

Humph was satisfied that he had his Eve back. Higgins, on the other hand, had nothing.

"If I may," he said, looking at Humph and nodding toward Eve.

It was as if the polite request jolted Humph awake. "Of course, of course. After all, I was the one who called you for this very reason."

Eve got up and poured herself another drink, then squeezed back in next to Humph on the sofa. She turned to face Higgins, who occupied the other end of the sofa.

"We thought you might have moved in with another mob guy," said Higgins, "or you were buttering up some union guy who was showing signs of selling himself to the mob for some reason or another. We kept checking with your director. He said you had stopped turning up for rehearsals. He said if the show was in the early days of preparation you would have been fired. Fortunately, he said, you have nailed the role. He would never let you go now."

Rebecca broke in to add:

"Damn right, guys. You should see her. She's a natural on stage."

Eve winked at her.

All eyes were now on Eve.

"Well, as my dad might tell you, I'm prone to both excitements and impatience. In Gagliardi's eyes I was small fish. He wasn't about to let a guppie swim with the big guys he would be using to pry open the various unions. I figured he had already taken aim at union guys for each Broadway union. To the best of my knowledge he only wanted to keep me around as something to nibble on while he enjoyed his evening martini."

Eve took a sip, then continued.

"So I bolted, telling him it was my time of the month and that I had affairs to tidy up."

"So where...?" Humph began.

"I was getting around to that, Dad. I decided the grass was greener on the other side, the good side. I'm a member of UA, United Artists. We're the biggest union in the Broadway brotherhood. I asked myself who would know most about our financial situation at present, who would know what to expect from each union officer, who would know most about what our faithful investors were encountering as a new contract approaches.

"I went to the top, to our union's chief financial officer. It took some deception to be allowed to meet with him. He doesn't usually deal with hoofers, especially who show up at his office door with skirts as short as the one I just happened to be wearing that day."

Long story short, Eve said, the guy claimed he had only a few minutes free.

"I ended up staying half the night. I went back to the theater and slept in a dressing room. I was gone before rehearsals started the next day. I didn't want to go home in case Gagliardi's boys had been sent to track me."

Higgins was not an afficionado of the theater and he was on the verge of urging Eve to dispense with the chronological narrative and explain what she had learned from the financial guy.

"In short, detective, at first he dismissed out of hand my suggestion that there was growing evidence that the mob might be about to attempt a takeover of our unions. I assured him I had come to him as a proud union member, one who was fully aware of our history of labor harmony, so much appreciated by members and investors alike. I then said time was too short before our next contract to sit around hoping to find breadcrumbs, signs of mob attempts to hijack our unions."

After a silence, Higgins said that Eve's approach was clever. He never would have thought of it himself. And not being a beautiful union member in a short skirt, he could never have pulled it off.

"Did this lord of finance respond?"

"It was early evening by the time I'd won him over. The giveaway was that he poured me a cognac. I'd never had one before, despite having spent much of my life in strip clubs and being entertained by ridiculously horny men."

Humph had grown used to hearing her talk about her days in burlesque, stripping and prostitution. He had learned to love the fact that she never revealed any embarrassment. She had dealt with what the cards dealt her. As she spoke, he looked at Higgins's face. He was disappointed to see no shock or embarrassment.

Eve continued.

"As I enjoyed my cognac, he made several phone calls. To whom, I don't know but they were obviously union people. Since normally my guy wouldn't be dealing with people far down the ladder, I assume he was speaking to union execs. You know, guys who had been elected by the membership. At one point he exploded, as much as well-bred guys like him explode. He said, 'Why the hell didn't you tell me.'"

She said what the union exec never told his ultimate boss was that he'd been offered $50,000 to tell our union members to reject any contract we were offered. He said he'd been told by the guy who offered the bribe that there was a Broadway revolution on the horizon.

"Once it was over, he said, we'd all be sitting pretty, more so than we'd ever dreamed. The spiel was that there was more money than we could imagine in the pockets of the guys who invest in shows. It was time we got our proper share."

"Once my guy heard that he wanted to rain hellfire on every crooked union exec. He got so absorbed in making furious phone calls he didn't even notice when I reached for his precious Cognac bottle and helped myself to a Lower East Side serving."

Higgins loved every detail of Eve's account.

"Now, what I need are names," he said.

Eve smiled at him, then reached under her bra and pulled out a raggedy piece of paper with pencil notations.

"You'll find the names of each exec my man called, including the ones who admitted receiving the $50,000 offer."

Higgins spent the longest time perusing the list.

Finally Higgins said:

"I sent out an entire squad of detectives seeking exactly this kind of information and, pardon me, Eve, a dance hall girl spends two days and comes up with conclusive proof of the mob's intentions. I'm so pissed off, utterly pissed off, and so joyous. Young woman, you should become chief of detectives. Unfortunately, you wouldn't be allowed to wear skirts like the one that seduced our main witness."

CHAPTER 30

IN the next three days, the NYPD spoke to each union executive who had been contacted by mob members. The gangsters, trying to seem friendly, had provided phone numbers for the union guys to call if they needed more information. The cops now put those numbers to good use, calling the mobsters Gagliardi had assigned to bring the unions into the fold. The cops pretended to be union guys. They set up meetings with them all, ensnaring each and every one.

Higgins was on cloud nine. Hearing the news the next day, his detective squad was relieved but most decided to keep a low profile anyway. It was not their finest hour. Their No. 1 suspect turned out to be the heroine of the day.

The problem that remained was how to nail a mob biggie. They knew Gagliardi, who they now knew sent out guys to put the squeeze on union execs. But they had to link Gagliardi's boss, none other than the so-called mayor of Bensonhurst, Salvatore Maranzano, Little Caesar, to the plot to control Broadway.

On their side was the already documented fact that Maranzano was behind the great mob war that year, instigated by him by inviting two of Al Capone's hit men to come to New York and rub out Don Vito Corleone, who had dared insist Maranzano give up his monopoly of New York gambling. The fact that 1933 had already become the worst year in the history of mob-union violence in the city's history added weight to the NYPD's evidence.

Over the following month, no new details surfaced. The initial joy within the NYPD had subsided.

In the meantime, Humph and Rebecca had almost become a couple. She had almost succeeded in erasing his suspicious nature, one that was so developed that it even applied to blind men soliciting funds on the street.

Unbeknownst to Humph, she had returned to Harlem, where they had started their investigation of Murder No. 1. Near where they first started looking in East Harlem, she found a young Hispanic couple, newly arrived in the country. She and the woman of the house chatted a while. The woman seemed happy to talk to another Spanish-speaker. Rebecca invited her for coffee. She accepted.

They went to a café on 93rd Street in West Harlem, previously Italian, newly Porto Rican. She was a sweet girl. Big dreams filled her head but Rebecca knew America offered little to fulfill them.

Rebecca mentioned the handsome black actor who got murdered not so long ago.

"The Haitian boy?"

She knew of him right away. Why?

"I'm not sure. He said he was supposed to give up his membership in the union. I don't know why or anything about that. He was supposed to convince other actors to do the same. All I know was what a friend told me. Anyway, he refused to turn on the union. The actor thought he was being well treated for his acting. Then he was killed. Just like that!"

Rebecca phoned Det. Higgins and told him that prior to the Haitian's death, someone told him that he had to start encouraging his fellow actors to quit the union. He refused and died because of it." She said she still had no information about the other two murders of actors.

Higgins was stunned once again by what a non-detective had uncovered, and even more amazing, two women. He was still in awe of Eve's accomplishment. And even more shamed by the performance of his own detectives. Two young women were putting the whole department to shame.

Rebecca said the young woman she just talked to was able to describe the man who visited the Haitian. She didn't see him personally but her friend said he had a face you'd never forget. The entire left side of his face was scarred. It was more purple than white.

Higgins settled himself down and thanked Rebecca profusely, not something Higgins was inclined to do normally. Then he asked:

"We canvassed that area thoroughly. Why, Rebecca, why would she tell you all that and not us?"

Rebecca switched to WASP mode and said plainly:

"If you're white, the door doesn't open in this part of town."

Rebecca was amazed that the NYPD, white to the core, had not learned that lesson.

"I'm beginning to think that's a lesson we need to learn, and damned fast. This city is changing overnight," said Higgins.

"You got it, sir."

Higgins smiled at the "sir".

Instead of going home, Rebecca headed to Humph's

place. She wanted to tell him about her discovery, especially since she and Humph started the investigation in East Harlem. She also wanted to cuddle with him. She was so deeply involved in what had become a gigantic investigation involving multiple murders, the mob and an American institution, Broadway, that she had become uncomfortable drifting alone in the underbelly of New York. All she wanted was to be the best make-up artist on Broadway.

When she arrived, Humph swept her up in his arms. He had never been that demonstrative. Before she had a chance to say, "Yeah but what the hell are you…", he planted a kiss on her that silenced all commentary.

Finally she said, "Are you the Humph I met months ago?"

He laughed.

"Quite possibly not."

Less than a minute after they consummated their relationship, a loud knock on the door shattered heaven.

Humph approached the door.

"What!" he shouted.

"What? I'll tell you what. MA-RAN-ZANO!"

Humph pulled the door open. It was Det. Mulroney.

Humph stepped aside to let him in.

"I get it," Mulroney said sensing the size of his interruption. "Bad time. But essential."

Humph looked into his front room. Rebecca had pulled on a dress.

"Sorry, ma'am," said Mulroney. Humph pointed to his table where chairs awaited.

The instant the detective was seated, he announced that Little Ceasar had been assassinated a few hours before.

"The gang war continues, Humph. That's fine if these mugs kill each other but we wanted to get Little Caesar in a courtroom. He could save his own skin by describing the whole effort to take over Broadway."

"Why would he do that?" asked Humph.

"Because thanks to your lady friend we know that he ordered the hit on the Haitian actor for refusing to reject the union. And we know that Gagliardi and he had an intense walk-and-talk just before the boy was killed. I suspect that Gagliardi himself did the deed to prove his commitment to Little C's grand plan."

Humph stood and paced, each hand vigorously scrubbing a side of his skull in the hope of generating enough circulation to produce a what-next thought.

When he finally sat again, he first asked whether Maranzano's demise meant the take-over plot had been extinguished. Case closed. Or, ..." He stood again, looking into the eyes of Rebecca, then Mulroney.

"Or does Gagliardi, who loves to pretend he's the city's greatest theatrical entrepreneur, believe he can pull this off on his own?"

Rebecca didn't say yes or no to Humph's suggestion. She merely added that her few days next to Gagliardi revealed he had Brooklyn's biggest ego.

"My instinct," said Mulroney, "tells me that while Gagliardi focused on Broadway, that ego you people mentioned would make the idea of replacing Maranzano irresistible. He'd love to be the head chef for all the illegal dealings Little Cesear had controlled. So what if he wasn't Sicilian-born. He saw himself as unbearably handsome and daring with more brights than anyone else."

Rebecca added support to the detective's argument. The first time Humph and I investigated him was when he tried to take over a Latin-dance hotspot in Harlem. He had the nerve to try to say his entrepreneurial genius would make him the ideal owner. I won't waste your time telling you how his absurd offer was received in Harlem by the Latino community. It was basically, 'No way, never.'"

She added: "It took one hell of an ego to go up there and propose that. He would have died had he heard what those Latinos were saying about the arrogant gringo after he left."

Mulroney then said he wasn't sure about the next step to take in their investigation.

"With the assassination of a major mob figure there's going to be a major battle for control of his interests. This case now goes beyond our precinct. All I can say right now, Rebecca, is to stay out of it. Stick to make-up or stick to Humph. You and Eve have given us the weapons we need to kick the crap out of organized crime. Now retire, please, please. Humph, make sure it happens."

CHAPTER 31

DETECTIVES talked at length with the Actors' Equity financial officer. He had contacts galore in the industry and, more specifically, names, addresses and phone numbers for all union executives. Within a week, the NYPD had statements from them all, clearly pointing to bribery and threats to all by goons clearly acting on orders from Gagliardi. Within two weeks, they'd arrested the mob guys who'd done the threatening. Together with interviews of union members, they had amassed a concerted effort to undermine the unions. Once they explained what they'd learned from Actors' Equity, the doors opened with all Broadway unions. A total of 11 union executives were subsequently charged with violating contractual conditions and attempting to undermine legal contracts.

The investigation then focused on the investors of all upcoming shows and even those that hadn't yet approached the Broadway League to invest in a new show. The cops discovered that several of them had more than questionable sources of investment money, companies that had never operated in New York or been granted contracts by the city.

Higgins followed their investigations closely. Humph phoned him daily for updates. He was not happy being on the sidelines.

Years before, Humph had befriended a secretary at a brokerage on Wall Street. The day before, they had met by accident on Bowling Green. Humph had been walking out his frustrations and was sweating more than he wanted. He sat and looked south toward the sea entrance to New York. From this viewpoint the city seemed great. Once inside, he knew it gnawed away at souls. A lot of immigrants, hundreds of thousands, got the hell out and returned to Europe. Though he was a born-and-bred New Yorker, someone probably incapable of living elsewhere, Humph often thought they were the lucky ones.

Out of nowhere, a voice called, "Humph! My man Humph!"

It took a moment but he suddenly recognized her.

"Gloria!"

She threw herself against him and exclaimed, "You're the only hero I know!"

"What in heaven's name are you talking about?"

She stepped back from the hug and grinned hugely as if their meeting up was a game.

"Don't you read the papers?"

"Of course I do."

"The *New York Times* has a piece about you today."

"About me? Why would they ever write about me?"

"They said you brought down a mob kingpin. Little Cesear. The paper said you learned that he ordered a hit on a young actor who was refusing to undermine some

238

Broadway union or another."

"Where in heaven's name would they have gotten that kind of information?"

"From the cops? From someone you know? I don't know. Who cares?"

Humph's only thought was that the paper's story placed a bullseye on his head. Not only were Eve and Rebecca at risk but so was he.

"They even published your picture."

"Where did they get my damned photo?" Humph was ready to take off running.

Gloria grabbed him and kept repeating, "Worry not, worry not."

Humph said, "You don't understand a thing!"

"But I do, Humph, I do."

"How!" Humph shouted.

"They've written about you before, Humph. You cracked that big case six or seven years ago. It took them a while but they investigated what you did and ended up asking why the hell can't the NYPD accomplish what you did? You should read the *Times* now and then."

"Are you doing promotion for the paper?"

Gloria laughed.

"No, you stubborn flatfoot."

Humph told her to stop and listen.

"I may have played a small roll in uncovering the fact that Little Ceasar had the young actor snuffed out but I had nothing to do with his demise. Don Vito Corleone is the one to thank for that. He wanted Little Ceasar to stop keeping all the take from gambling operations. He then imported two hitmen from Chicago and they did the dirty deed. No more Maranzano. They were on their way out of town by the time Maranzano's body hit the sidewalk."

Gloria had listened as ordered. As Humph started to move away she demanded to know where he was going.

"I want to see what lies *The Times* wrote."

"No need, Humph." Gloria rolled up the paper that had been under her arm and tossed it the way a delivery boy would to Humph, 10 feet away. "Let's go sit. I want to watch your face as you read the story."

She was teasing him and he wasn't in the mood. He scrunched his big left hand around the paper and made an abrupt right turn into Battery Park. He looked for a bench closest to the harbor. Manhattan and its gangsters and corrupt politicians were behind him, out of sight, out of mind. He often went there, some days facing the Hudson River, other days Liberty Island and eventually the ocean.

He crossed his legs and opened the paper, turning the pages until he heard Gloria's voice:

"Page 12, Humph. Under the headline, 'Busted on Broadway.'"

He jerked around. He didn't know she was behind him, standing, with a smirk only the evil-hearted could manage.

He snapped open the page so hard he almost tore it.

Humph found no untruths in the first half of the story. He began to relax until he spotted his name and a tiny photo that Higgins must have dug out of the file on Humph when he was a copper. Higgins had been quoted earlier in the story and the paper ran his picture as well.

He read on...

"Mr. Higgins, chief of detectives at the main Lower East Side Precinct station, was effusive in his praise for outsiders more so than his own investigators. Even more unusual, Mr. Higgins insisted on underlining the role played by two women, neither of them on the force."

"'Not only was it highly unusual but those two young ladies practically laid the case at our feet. They took all the risks and they produced the missing link to the puzzle. Because the mob is involved, and considering what they revealed in terms of evidence against certain mob members, in particular Walton Gagliardi, I believe them to be still in danger. This is my reason for refusing to name them for this story.'"

Humph was relieved.

"Well done, Higgins," he mumbled. Gloria, still standing behind Humph, put a hand on his shoulder. She knew what he had just read. However she felt Humph's shoulders stiffen as he read on:

"Mr. Higgins went on to inform our reporter that a private eye who is well-known in this city as simply Humph, a bastardization of Humphrey, his real first name, set the ball rolling. 'The girls worked under his guidance more than mine. Humph attended all our detective squad meetings. He's a man who possesses a rare quality for a New Yorker. He prefers listening to talking. The fact is that he and one of the ladies in question started investigating the real bad guy in this affair long before the NYPD knew there was anything to investigate. By the time we became aware that something big was afoot, Humph and his assistant were able to set the stage for us. They hoped we would solve it. We didn't get far. Then the two ladies, with Humph behind them, called me at home late one night and insisted I visit them at a meeting place they had designated near Tompkins Square. They told me their theory that explained everything, then lo and behold, the very next day a gangland assassination bore out everything they'd said.'"

The reporter quoted Higgins one more time.

"'This city has honored Humph previously, after he solved a complex case of murder, bootlegging and smuggling in 1927. In my opinion, sir, it is time we did so again, this time including his two clever and courageous assistants.'"

Humph leaned back on the bench and with a smile handed the paper back to Gloria.

"Not too painful, Humph?"

"No, not at all. In fact..."

Gloria cut him off.

"I also brought along two of our boldest tabloid papers

from this morning. Worry not, detective, they don't betray your girls. However they do explain your accomplishment better than you ever would be willing to."

The first paper's Page 1 headline screamed:

"BROADWAY SAVED"

The other paper announced:

"Great White Way Still Shines Bright".

Both papers had realized what no one had spoken of aloud. The mob attempt at taking over Broadway unions had been well under way and in no time at all the Gagliardi-led invasion would have destroyed one of America's greatest institutions. They said the mob had already invaded Hollywood. Both efforts were aimed at mob control of investment in new shows and movies and profits.

One paper said, "The same lowlifes who run gambling and prostitution and untold other obscenities in our city would control the place of dreams and joy that keeps our heads above water in these frightful times of despair."

The other paper concluded:

"Broadway is New York. New York is Broadway."

They both reminded readers that the noble union movement that began in New York and spread across the country had been viciously compromised by the mob, threatening the survival of industry itself.

The second tabloid ended its story with:

"May we, as New Yorkers, always happily bring to our lips the song 'Give my regards to Broadway.'"

Humph sat motionless for at least three minutes. Suddenly, he rose to his feet. He walked toward Gloria and extended his arms like airplane wings. He hugged her and laughed loudly.

"Damn you," he said. "You set me up for a scare. You knew all along that we were no longer in danger."

Her big grin acknowledged her subterfuge.

"Now go see your girls."

CHAPTER 32

ONCE the papers had hit the street, Eve's show gave her the day off from rehearsal. As for Rebecca, she almost got fired for spontaneously applying other-worldly make-up to the show's lead. She explained to the stage director that she couldn't help it. It was a creative outburst, she said, pent-up energy from the fight to save Broadway. She got a pat on the behind and an order to take the week off. She almost retaliated for the former but realized the director had been under pressure as well. He wouldn't get a second pass.

As for Humph, he wasn't happy that he couldn't reach either girl the day he read the papers. By early evening, he had given up. He'd phoned Duffy.

"Read the papers, Duff?"

"Never read 'em. Nothin' but nonsense."

"Agree completely. Get you Irish ass over here now."

They drank until dawn,

Six months later, Duffy was dragged to City Hall to receive his award.

Two special ladies were in the front row. They were asked to join Humph, who was already on stage. Humph thought this would be the highlight of his life, here at City Hall, the mayor in front of him, Eve holding his right hand, Rebecca his left.

Then the photographers' cameras started flashing like battlefield flak.

"Get me home, Eve. Get me home."

She smiled and bowed her head at those applauding. Rebecca launched a haughty smile and as she and her long legs strode offstage.

The men in the audience gawked, open mouthed.

On the way to Humph's place in a taxi, Eve couldn't help reflecting on the case that led to her award and the 1927 case that almost cost her her life.

"Everything's so damned messed up in this city," she said aloud. "Things will never change. Corruption on top of corruption."

"Perhaps they will change someday," said Humph. "You and Rebecca just improved the odds."

ABOUT THE AUTHOR

Wayne Clark is a Montreal writer and author
of five other New York-based novels, including the
international award-winning literary fiction novel *he
& She*. In addition to writing fiction he has worked
as a journalist, copywriter and translator.

www.ingramcontent.com/pod-product-compliance
Lightning Source LLC
Chambersburg PA
CBHW051339020726
47501CB00007B/2162